THE ELEVENTH COMMANDMENT

RHYS HUGHES

The Eleventh Commandment and Other Very Short Fictions

Copyright © 2025 by Rhys Hughes

The Eleventh Commandment and Other Very Short Fictions is a work of fiction. Any references to historical events, real people, or real locales are used fictitiously. Other names, characters, places, and incidents are the product of the author's imagination, and any resemblance to actual events or locales or persons, living or dead, is entirely coincidental.

Cover and title page design by Bryan Maloney
Back cover author photo by Maithreyi Karnoor

Print ISBN: 979-8-9886702-3-0

Library of Congress Control Number: 2025938948

RECITAL PUBLISHING
Woodstock, NY
www.recitalpublishing.com

Recital Publishing is an imprint of the online podcast The Strange Recital.
Fiction that questions the nature of reality
www.thestrangerecital.com

Contents

The Zodiacal Light

Aries — 3

Taurus — 6

Gemini — 9

Cancer — 11

Leo — 13

Virgo — 16

Libra — 19

Scorpio — 21

Ophiuchus — 24

Sagittarius — 27

Capricorn — 29

Aquarius 31

Pisces 33

Beyond Necessity

Kafka's Birthday 37

One Mighty Bound 38

Kissing With Noses 39

Teachers 40

In the Corner 41

Fever 42

Occam's Beard 43

Shadow Foot 45

Baldness 46

Listening to Leonora 47

The Contrast 48

The Leg Puppies 49

When I Discovered Laziness 50

Frankenstein Films 52

The Giant Woman 53

Exaggeration 54

In the Den with Daniel 55

Big Enough   57

The Skull   58

A Man on Stilts   59

How Cold is It?   62

Anatole France   63

The Birds   65

Postmodern Picnic   66

The Leaves   68

Stretching My Legs   70

Do They Believe?   71

The Mirror   72

The Underwater Trapeze   73

The Eleventh Commandment   74

The Façade   76

The Ventriloquist   78

The Gorgon   80

The Fireman   81

Infinity Gears   82

Walking the Wrong Plank   84

The Sea and the Ruins   86

Inside the Minotaur   87

The Prison   88

Head in Hands   90

The Windmill   91

Alexander Kluge   92

Washing Our Hands   94

How to Wake Up   95

The Umbrella   96

Song of the Sirens   98

The Slipper Exchange   100

The Palace   101

Pressed Flowers   106

The Octopus and the Clock   108

My Swiss Neighbour   109

The Palace Coup   110

Whirlwind Romance   114

The Witch   116

A Deep Breath   119

The Tired Bed   120

The Illuminations   121

The Ostraca of Inclusion

Beyond the Edge 125

The Book Burning 127

Unwanted in Paradise 129

A Room With a View 131

White Cliffs 133

Map of Conquest 136

Just A Second 139

The Eclipse Flower 141

Monsieur Choux 143

Tumble Keys 145

Nostalgia City 147

Freight of Years 150

The Lamp 153

The Wardrobe of Love 155

The Lost Coffee 158

The Möbius Minutes 160

The Mirrors 163

The Overdue Book 165

About the Author 169

A Request 170

Other Books from Recital Publishing 171

This book is dedicated to
Maithreyi Karnoor

The Zodiacal Light

The zodiacal light is very faint and so are we, from hunger, a hunger for the stars, the stars we can never reach. Yes, it is faint and so are our hopes, but that doesn't matter if we enjoy the standing and reaching, on the shoulders of our friends, on a ladder, on chairs piled on chairs. We are nearer the stars that way. The zodiacal light is a cone of glow that extends from the horizon and along the constellations of astrology. It is a false dawn, but any dawn is better than none.

Aries

I HAD NEVER TAKEN astrology seriously and in many ways I still don't, but Octavia was good at changing the minds of men. She dressed in a very anachronistic way but the eyes that saw her soon came to believe that modernity is overrated. She insisted that the stars really did influence our fates.

"They also control what happens to inanimate objects."

"Don't be absurd," I protested.

She swished the hem of her toga and smirked.

"What zodiac sign are computers?"

I shrugged at the question.

"Aries, of course. The Ram," as if this was enough.

"I don't believe you."

Later we went for a walk in the park. It was a spring day and the sunlight pushed through the branches of the trees like honey. I bathed in the glow, but Octavia pulled my sleeve and soon we were running towards the lake. She wanted to hire a boat and row across to the other side. So I said:

"What will you be doing while I work the oars?"

"Playing music," she replied.

I frowned at this because she had brought no instruments with her. We selected a rowing boat and clambered inside. The attendant cast off a rope. I pulled on the oars and we glided towards the centre of the lake. A mist rose unexpectedly from the cool waters and it was so thick I could see nothing, not even Octavia who sat facing me on the wooden bench. I kept rowing.

The mist cleared and now I saw that she had a large drum between her knees and two thick drumsticks to beat it with.

At the same time I felt a coldness around my ankles.

I was shackled to my bench.

My chains rattled as I tugged at them.

"Don't stop," she said.

Then she began to beat the drum with powerful strokes. An instinct compelled me to take up the oars again and resume rowing. I rowed in time to her rhythm. Ahead of us another boat came into view, an easy target.

Octavia increased the tempo of her playing. Her toga slipped from her shoulders and I could almost taste her bare olive skin. Her perspiration glittered like jewels on her forehead and on her full lips, each droplet containing a tiny rainbow. I strained to pull the oars as hard as I possibly could.

"Ramming speed!"

Ah, that ram again. So boats at war were also born under the sign of Aries. That made a certain amount of sense. I saw that the enemy boat contained a businessman who was operating a laptop computer. He was being rowed by a man in the uniform of a chauffeur. We would sink them both.

It was early afternoon and the empire was thriving.

Beneath our boat I was aware of sunken vessels and broken computers and also the bones of other men, all entangled with weeds and kissed by fish. What sign are fish born under? I didn't need to ask. The bones poked through holes in rotten wool cardigans and that was the important thing. Woollen clothes dyed a softly glowing golden colour in the vats of my nostalgia.

Taurus

"WHAT SIGN DO YOU think the minotaur is?"

This was an unexpected question from above. I turned my head and saw him three floors above, leaning out of his window. I was watering the flowers in their boxes on the balcony and I stood up slowly and stretched. Then I paid serious attention to the question and finally said, "Taurus."

He nodded. It was the obvious answer, but his nod was ironic and it was clear he was disagreeing with me. It occurred to me that maybe the body of the minotaur and his head would have different birthdays and be born under two different signs, but I was in no mood for riddles and shrugged.

"Do you suppose he was attracted to women or cows?"

"I beg your pardon?"

"The minotaur! Were his amorous desires determined by his human mind or his bovine physicality? I can't work it out."

"You seem very interested in the details of his life."

"Don't be absurd, he never lived."

"Yes, he was a myth only."

"Nonetheless, he was born under the sign of Taurus."

"But that's what I said earlier."

"Oh, did you? I misheard. I thought you said 'torus', which as we both know is a geometrical shape and not a zodiac sign."

My neighbour was a joker, of this I was certain now. I wondered why we hadn't interacted until this moment. I spend a lot of time on my balcony and he must have seen me there. I leaned on the railings and looked down on the city. The old alleys and narrow streets were like a maze. The thread that would lead a lost traveller out again was made from air, only the wind.

It was perfectly possible for the minotaur to have escaped the labyrinth by chance, from wandering at random, and in this case Theseus would have found it empty when he ventured inside, but for the sake of saving face his story wouldn't change. Nobody could dispute that he slew the creature. Yet the monster was free, making his way in a world where he must always be alone.

No woman could want him, nor any cow. Never settling down, he would voyage to the edge of the known world and who can say what he would do when he reached it? Sit on his haunches and wait, I guess.

My neighbour had a man's head, not that of a bull, so he couldn't be the minotaur, as I briefly suspected when he asked me a third question, "Who does he support in a bullfight, the beast or the matador?" and I said, "The answer depends less on the fact he's a hybrid than on his sense of justice."

"Meaning what exactly?"

"Anyone with a sense of justice supports the bull."

"I am his descendant, you see."

"How is that feasible?"

"Somewhere on this remarkable planet of ours he must have met a woman with a cow's head. Over many generations the bovine aspects weakened. All that remains is my unusual stomach. I don't complain."

Before I could raise an objection, he added wistfully:

"A shame I don't exist."

Gemini

THEY WERE TWINS AND they went down the street arm in arm and I never saw either of them without the other. Absolutely identical in appearance, of course, but one was on roller skates and the other just wore ordinary shoes and had to run to keep up with her sister. I would sit at the cafe terrace and they would pass over my shadow, one rolling and the other loping, and I wasn't sure whether to feel amused or disturbed. Not once did I attempt to speak to them. It would have felt dissolute. I merely sipped my coffee and watched them recede into the distance.

When I stood up from my seat later I noticed that my shadow had trouble freeing itself from the pavement, as if it had been pressed into the slabs, and it took a wrench of my shoulders to prise it loose This happened every time and I got into the habit of shrugging theatrically before departing the cafe and then setting off along a road that was at a tangent to the one the sisters had taken. If I didn't shrug to unstick it, but just walked away, perhaps it would snap completely off at the point where it met my feet. I was reluctant to risk so odd an eventuality.

Yet there is probably no more effective way of keeping a favourite chair free at a cafe than by leaving one's shadow alongside. Unlike a coat, nobody is going to steal the thing. But I couldn't bear to forsake my shadow by neglecting to shrug, walking off alone, abandoning it like an elongated kitten that one has neither the time nor the patience for. As for damage to the shadow itself, yes I'm sure there was plenty of that, but it is difficult to see bruises on a totally dark object. In fact, what is a shadow but a nullity of substance, light and information?

As for the twins, I'm no expert at astrology but it was clear to me they were born under the sign of Gemini. They had a certain air about them that convinced me I was right on this point. I decided to research that constellation and so I discovered that the two brightest stars it contains are named Castor and Pollux, the twins of mythology who were born from an egg. Their mother was Leda and she laid the egg after Zeus visited and ravished her in the form of a swan. This actually told me very little about the two girls. But then I had an inspiration.

I was at home in my study. I dropped my pen and it rolled under the desk and my arm wasn't long enough to retrieve it. I had no option but to move the desk and to my relief this proved an easy task. The desk was mounted on little wheels. It rolled across the floorboards smoothly, accelerating towards the open door and the stairs beyond. I had visions of it crashing down the steps and smashing itself to pieces. So I held onto it and ran next to it. We were just like twins hurrying along a street, the important one mounted on castors, and never mind the Pollux.

Cancer

WALKING ALONG THE BEACH I understood that I had gone in a complete circle around the island. There were the footprints I had left behind when I set off. The tide hadn't yet filled them. This meant the island was rather small, but I already knew this, didn't I? I looked down at my bare feet and said:

"The prints are those of a man wearing sandals."

But let's not jump to conclusions.

If one jumps in any way whatsoever on a beach, the prints will be even harder to interpret the next time you see them. The fact I wasn't wearing sandals now had little bearing on the issue. I might have worn them out on my circular walk, eroded them to nothing, exposing my toes shamelessly.

The obvious way of finding out for sure would be to follow these prints and keep them under close observation. My idea was that gradually they would change into the prints of a man with bare feet. The process would be interesting to observe. Sandals aren't monstrous and neither are feet, but some midway stage might be dreadful, the prints would resemble those of a demon.

A beach demon in this subtropical paradise, this isolated speck of land lost upon a mighty ocean, this refuge of the shipwrecked sailor, the castaway passenger, the lost and battered stowaway on a cruise ship. We all know many legends of the sea. Beneath the waves lurk mermaids and monsters.

I followed the prints and in fact I matched them step for step, my bare feet fitting easily into the indentations. It seemed I was wearing invisible and intangible sandals, but there was no one to see this, and even witnesses wouldn't have been able to form any important judgements about them.

As I went along, I found myself admiring the person who had made the prints in a totally objective way. There was no hint of narcissism in this appreciation. The man who made them was an abstract concept. I had forgotten my ego at some point on the sands of this second circumnavigation.

And yes, the prints began to change, to melt at the edges, to lose confidence in the certainty they were sandals. But they didn't become more footlike. On the contrary I was dismayed to see them contract like pools of water draining through a hole in the world but smaller, until they were points.

There were more of them too. At last they left the beach and veered inland and so I followed them, walking sideways, almost scuttling, through the coconut palms and up the rocky slope of the extinct volcano at the very centre of the island. At the summit I sat on a black boulder to catch my breath.

A shipwrecked man must catch his own breath for every meal. The view was quite tremendous. It was shocking. The island was shaped exactly like a giant crab. It was threatening the ocean with its pincers. I looked at my reflection in the shiny obsidian and what I saw was a body without a sole.

Leo

"THAT'S A NICE NAME, a name I have always liked. It is regal and strong and yet there's something cute about it too. I imagine you like to be cuddled, especially at night. Too much cuddling and you will snarl and that will be amusing, because you won't bite at all, just pretend to. To ruffle your hair must be fun also. When you are caught out in the rain and shake your head I bet the displaced droplets scatter far and wide. I could read a long book at night by the reflected shine from your perfectly white teeth. You are a wonderful person, I can tell this already."

"Thanks for the compliments."

"But you aren't entirely happy with my words?"

"It's not that, oh no."

"You don't have an issue with compliments?"

"None whatsoever."

"Yet you wish I hadn't spoken?"

"Only because I'm wondering if it's entirely appropriate for my co-pilot to concern himself with such matters just before take-off.

If you had waited until we were safely up in the air, I would think it less strange."

"Apologies, captain."

"Call me Leo…"

Just a routine flight, of course, and completely uneventful, up into the clouds and through them and over them. The aeroplane cast its shadow on the tops of banks of cumulus tufts and I watched it hurry across that snowfield in the sky, my face pressed against the cold glass of the tiny window, and I wondered what would happen if the shadow decided to fly somewhere else. Not to accompany us but to diverge and land in some other land. Would our passenger shadows disembark there or would they be unable to vacate their non-existent seats?

Around the shadow of our aeroplane was a perfectly circular rainbow that rippled and undulated over the irregularities in the surface of the clouds but never broke off and always kept pace. It was charming. We all know there is a pot of gold at the end of the rainbow, gold as yellow and dangerous as a healthy lion, but this rainbow had no end. It was sealed all the way around. Then we left all the clouds behind and flew over the savanna and it was possible to see lions down there. They were the gold and they were the pots that gripped the gold.

Why was I flying to Africa at this time in my life? There is never a wrong time to do so, that's the answer. The lion that the constellation Leo is named after had nothing to do with Africa. It lived in Nemea in Greece but originally fell from the moon. One must be very foolish and extremely tough to fall from the moon and land unscathed in a rocky country. But its fur was impenetrable. And now the aeroplane begins its long descent and

we are falling not from the moon but sliding out of the blue, and
Captain Leo is in full control, confident, majestic.

Virgo

The purity of the untouched man or woman.

We wonder if this is a dangerous condition. Avoiding life isn't really purity but an amateurish rehearsal for death. The actors find it difficult to learn their lines. The old theatre is draughty and morosely decays.

A building with weeds on the outer sills of all the windows. But that doesn't look too bad, to be honest, it gives the place a verdant charm. Some of the weeds are able to produce flowers that nod in the breeze.

At some point the wind chills itself seeking entrance.

It scrapes off its warmth in the cracks.

A leaner and meaner current of air remains to circulate horribly down the sagging passages of the vintage pile, that crumbling music hall where a drama society meets once a week to prepare for an opening night.

I help to set up and control the lights. I am a volunteer.

The play is a very old one.

It is about unsullied women forced to marry conquering warriors. It is one of the most ancient plays in existence. But none of us knows how to pronounce the name of its author correctly. On our lips Aeschylus trips. I narrow the beam of a spotlight and illuminate the mouth of the director.

"You need to put more feeling into it, more feeling."

He fans dust with the script.

Glances are exchanged in a way that virginities can never be. Of all the plays the society might have chosen, why this one? A light modern comedy would have been a finer choice. There will be an audience anyway, of course, comprising the family and friends of the performers, just them.

There's a hole in the ceiling directly above my head.

I look up and see the sky.

One of the magnifying lenses for the lights is resting by my side. I pick it up and hold it to my eye like an absurd monocle.

Indoors, but I am outside.

That's how decayed the roof is, the tiles have peeled away, as if time is an uncut fingernail and the theatre is a tangerine. I see a star, a single point of light, and with a frown I wonder if it is really a star. Not all stars are stars. Some are planets that only look like stars. My eyesight is sharp.

It might even be an asteroid shining up there.

This is highly unlikely, I know, but not entirely impossible. There are at least two asteroids that on rare occasions might be seen through binoculars from the surface of our own world. Ceres and Vesta.

Both of them are named after goddesses.

I feel intensely aristocratic as I remain with my monocle in place and the director on the stage below rants his nonsense.

Vesta above me, her virgins below, the Vestal virgins.

But I am not at all like them.

I lower the lens to the floor, unbutton my shirt and take it off. I fling it at the hole in the ceiling and it passes through, caught by a gust like a sail. Off it goes on a most spontaneous flapping voyage, and I remain bare-chested in control of the lights, skin bristling, with no vest to cover the truth.

Libra

"Libra is the only zodiac sign that's an inanimate object," she remarked, and I didn't let her know that many people had already told me the same thing. Our knees touched and the contact thrilled me, sounding a chord in my soul, and I shivered and froze in position, my hands over the keyboard.

"Play me the scales I taught you," she said.

I felt small at that moment deep inside, but in fact I was never larger in my life, all the lifting down at the opera house had given me big muscles, shifting all that scenery every night before a performance, and my clothes hardly fitted me, but my touch was still delicate enough for what she asked.

Yet I was nervous in her presence and played wrong notes.

She wagged a finger and said:

"Just pretend I'm not here and do what I tell you."

"I am alone here, you mean?"

"Yes, perfect solitude."

"So how can you tell me anything?"

"Just with my mouth."

Then I was kissing her and she was kissing me, and I knew her mouth was there, despite my loneliness, and if her mouth was there the rest had to follow. We fell off the narrow piano stool onto the thick carpet. It was luxurious to roll across the room on it, tightly embraced, ending up near the window just as if the divine hand of love had played a passionate scale with us from one end to the other, and every note was a gasp of pleasure and sweet bafflement.

When we finally broke apart, I said, "I've never kissed a piano teacher," and she said, "I've never kissed a scenery shifter," and some equivalence was achieved from these confessions, but not before our words had gone up and down first. I told her it was just a question of scale, of scales, of weighing scales, and I was confused about which scales were which, but I remained happy with what had happened. And I was still a Libran, despite all the tumbling.

We propped ourselves on our elbows and looked out.

The city appeared distant, far below us, as if our building was rising high into the atmosphere, and my place of work, the opera house, seemed no larger than the fist of a baritone playing a jealous husband. Vertigo gripped me for a moment, then I noticed another building coming down as we went up. In the window of one of its rooms two faces peered back at us and I asked:

"What instrument is *he* learning, I wonder?"

"It doesn't matter," she said.

The scales are never truly at rest. To find the balance they seek they must oscillate endlessly. Soon we would be at the same altitude as the angels. Golden feathers shine in the sun but they aren't feathers as we know them. They are scales, and these angels swim through space like fish, while we attain the highest point, pause at the zenith for only an instant, and begin our return journey.

Scorpio

A STING IN THE tail, a tale to tell. In the desert one should always shake out one's shoes in the morning before putting them on. Scorpions like to hide there, probably thinking it is a cave. So how can we be sure, when we enter caves, that we aren't in fact going into the shoes of a gigantic alien entity that is camping overnight on our planet? Well, we can't and that's something to bear in mind.

The fire is burning low, the flame flickers out and now there are just embers that shift like the banks of lights of a primitive electronic adding machine. What can it be counting out here? Only the numbers of scorpions lurking under rocks as the desert rapidly cools. We have boiled water for coffee, we sip the bitter liquid gratefully and we squint at cactus shadows in the starlight.

"Always they look like assassins waiting for us to fall asleep."

"Yet those assassins must also make camp on their journey and they too will be threatened by the same cactus shadows."

"You are right. And what do the scorpions fear?"

"Oh, they have predators too."

Joe was a fine companion on such an expedition. He had a good name and a fine physique for this kind of thing. He was hardy. In fact his full name was Joe Hardy. A desert to him was no more disconcerting than a park would be to a mother. His pram was his cranium and his baby was all the knowledge he had about survival in a place where water is scarce and temperatures are erratic and loneliness is extreme, and he liked to wheel that pram up and down forever.

"I read once that in prehistoric times they had winged scorpions."

"Who had them?" I asked.

"They did, the other creatures. Think how unfair that was! Scorpions already are armoured, they have pincers and stings. To give them wings too seems a bit rich, as if nature is showing favouritism. A winged scorpion can do almost anything. It can fly and sting you in the eye, if it so chooses."

"But they went extinct?"

"Maybe lightning bolts fried them in their own husks."

"It's the only explanation."

The foot crushes the scorpion, the foot of history, the same foot that broke all the toes of prehistory by standing on them during the dance of time. But the sting of the scorpion gets its revenge, puncturing the skin of the ankle and killing the possessor of the foot. This is why socks were invented.

"A cactus is like the sock of a gigantic alien entity."

Joe nodded at this. "Bingo!"

I could tell what he was thinking when I said this. He was worried. He suspected I had rumbled him, and probably I would have, if only I knew what rumbling someone really meant. It is connected with thunder, I assume, the same thunder that applauded the zapping of those pesky flying scorpions. I finished my coffee and lay down in my blanket to sleep like a log in a treeless waste.

Ophiuchus

"THERE ARE THIRTEEN ZODIAC signs and this fact isn't well known but it is true anyway. I want to speak up for the constellation that is always forgotten. I know that the bulk of it doesn't lie on the apparent plane of the planets, that the sun and moon only scrape its southern edge, but nonetheless it deserves to be acknowledged for what it is. Yes, it's a perfectly valid astrological sign."

Before I could open my mouth to speak, the reply came:

"Ophiuchus is the name."

"The name of the sign or your name?"

"Both in a sense."

I had visited the carnival that was newly arrived in town. It was a wet day, a dour afternoon, and few people had bothered to wander among the tents and stalls. I was the only one to attend the performance of the snake charmer. He played a flute and a snake danced for him, but I saw that the snake was in fact a toy and connected to the end of the flute by a very thin wire.

He moved the flute as he played it and the snake swayed.

And the tent rippled too.

It had been erected too hastily. I don't think the pegs were secure in the ground, in the saturated earth, but I was amused by the show. It had cost only pennies anyway, I didn't feel cheated at all. How we had got onto the subject of astrology slips my mind now, unless it was because the charmer wore a gown spangled with symbols that may have been those of the mystical planets.

"Ophiuchus is the snake charmer in the sky?"

"Indeed it is," he replied.

"What are the attributes it confers?"

He frowned, perhaps because he didn't know, but he was a showman so he felt he ought to say something definite on the subject. He replaced his flute in the basket and lowered the wicker lid over it, then he shifted his weight, uncrossed his legs, leaned back on the cushion that served as his seat.

He rested his weight on one elbow and declared:

"People born under the sign of Ophiuchus generally don't know that they are and believe themselves to be either Scorpios or Sagittarians. Therefore they will always be bewildered that they have none of the qualities attributed to those other two signs. This will make them sceptical of astrology. They will become sceptical on all magical topics and they will disbelieve in Atlantis. This is a sadly ironic outcome because on the seabed somewhere, resting on a tumbled altar, a mermaid will be playing a watery flute for a sea snake, and daydreaming about life on land, on the mythical continents where those sceptics currently reside."

He sighed and added, "Disbelief is their main quality."

"I don't believe you," I said.

"That proves the point I am making."

"I don't believe it does."

He shrugged and smiled and I left his tent and squelched my way through mud to the next carnival attraction. The continents are not dry, not here at any rate, and that mermaid wouldn't feel too far from home. And how are mermaids born under stars at all? The light doesn't filter that far down.

Sagittarius

WHEN THE SKY IS clear at night and we peer at the constellation Sagittarius we are looking towards the centre of our own galaxy. Our solar system is maybe two-thirds of the way to the edge of intergalactic space, where it is not only terribly cold but horribly lonely. Once I stood on the edge of a continent and gazed across a sea that I couldn't swim in the direction of an unvisited landmass. Looking at other galaxies is just as futile but on a vastly grander scale.

It seems unlikely that spacecraft will ever be able to cross those gulfs from this island of stars to another spiral of suns, even if they are shaped like golden arrows fired from the bow of a god. Much better to turn our attention to the crowded part of the Milky Way where the stars jostle each other so closely that planets are plausibly shared between them in complicated orbits. That's what I did last night. I projected myself in my imagination across the void.

My body was a spacecraft and as I accelerated to impossible speeds, the stars that should have changed their colours remained white and hissed past me like the sparks of a campfire. The truth is that nothing in my experience had prepared me for flight at light speed in the pitiless vacuum. A failure of vision meant that the trip was more like a bicycle journey than a cosmic odyssey. I wondered what astrologers would say that astronomers would keep silent about.

With the bulk of the galaxy behind Sagittarius it's clear that gravity will exert lots more force from that direction than from any other of the zodiac signs. Sagittarius is thus the most powerful sign of all. Unless the forces that control fates have nothing to do with gravity. That's always a possibility. Then I remembered that I had a bow and arrows in my basement, a present from some friend or a souvenir from a holiday, who can say for sure? I went to retrieve them.

My window was wide open and I lifted the bow, nocked an arrow and pulled with all my might. I was no longer in full possession of my senses. The bow was steady in my grip and I knew I was aiming at the exact centre of our galaxy. The arrow would fly through Sagittarius harmlessly, missing all the stars, thudding into the black hole that is the fulcrum around which all the suns dance. What did I hope to achieve with the murder of the pivot of the Milky Way?

I released the string and the arrow sped into darkness. I closed the window and returned the bow to the basement. Then I sat in a chair to read a book but an hour or so later there was a knock on my door. I got up to open it and found myself facing a man with an arrow stuck through his tall hat. With a grimace that suited him not at all, he said, "I was drinking milk when the shock of the impact made me spill it down my shirt," but I had no statement to make.

That's just the way it was, the Milky Way it was.

Capricorn

THE GHOST OF A goat, that's what it was, and I saw it when I happened to glance out of the window. It was the middle of the night but the moon was full and I was thirsty. As I left the bed behind I felt an awful sense of loss, as if the bed was my childhood and would be grown up by the time I saw it next, perhaps ready to leave home or married with children. It was a ludicrous thought.

But I was half asleep still, a sleepwalker almost, shambling along the corridor that leads from bedroom to kitchen. My tongue felt like a bridge over a dry riverbed. The need to irrigate it was intense, but I paused anyway when I reached the grimy glass of that window and I glanced out, as I always do. It fascinates me, that window, because there's no acceptable reason why it's there.

It faces a blank wall. Only a blank wall confronts the viewer who looks through it and the blank wall is only a few inches away from the glass. But the moon was high and beams slid down the gap and they were enough. The window was full of a goat's face that was shining in the buttery beams and it smiled at me, that face. I know that such a beastly smile is always an illusion.

But I believed it anyway. I smiled back. Then I asked myself ferociously why was I so damn keen on being polite to ghosts, because it had to be a ghost, no living goat could manage to fit in that narrow space. I'm aware they are climbers of dexterity and endurance, but the wall was just too close.

To compensate for my smile I made a dismissive gesture. I pouted to demonstrate I was too busy for nonsense at this late hour, that I required water and not hairiness to help me sleep soundly until dawn, that acting the goat is childish, that the cottage had been rented for just one month, too bad.

In the kitchen I made a point of drinking two glasses of water, not one, in order to punish the ghost of the goat. Then I returned along the corridor to the bedroom. Yes, I looked through the window on the way back. The goat had vanished. There was only the brick wall, that looming brick wall.

With a violent shudder I realised how much more oppressive than the goat it was, a blankness, an oppression, a barrier that would never smile, even if it cracked in the most fortuitous manner. I recovered my composure and climbed back into bed. But I hugged my pillow and kissed it all over.

I waited fearfully to fall asleep. I knew that dreams would come. Nightmares are horses but deliriums can be goats. It occurred to me that the ghost was a brick in the wall that decided to evolve into the semblance of a living being. I stayed awake by remaining in deep love with my pillow.

Aquarius

THE WOMAN SCOOPED UP the water in her cupped palms and carried it across to the pot she wanted to boil for tea, but it poured through her fingers and landed on the slats of the bridge and trickled through the gaps and rained on the people below, who shouted up at her, "Watch what you're doing!"

"Oh, it's hard carrying water from a waterfall all the way across a swaying bridge to the spot I have chosen for a picnic."

"Why don't you take the kettle to the waterfall?"

"It's very heavy, that's why."

"Ask a helpful man to carry it for you."

"You don't understand. The bridge is an old one and can't take the extra weight, so I must carry the water two handfuls at a time. There's no other way. When my kettle is full I can boil it and brew tea."

"You tea drinkers are obsessive lunatics!"

"But fully refreshed ones."

The people below who shouted up were on the decks of passing boats and I felt a great deal of astonishment that they should be so troubled by a few drops of water. I thought the waterfall would splash a lot more liquid onto them as they sailed near it than had this silvery girl with the picnic that had already gone wrong. But maybe they can forgive a waterfall more easily.

There was only a little water left in her hands by the time she reached her kettle. I was enjoying my own picnic close to her spot. I was eating grapes and reading a book written more than a thousand years ago. I understood very little of it but the grapes were fully comprehensible. I said:

"Would you like some grapes instead of tea?"

"No, thank you. Because—"

I waited but the explanation never came. Or rather it was drowned out by a laugh so loud I thought a thunderstorm had started in the mountains. I turned to look and it was a daredevil in a canoe who had gone over the waterfall and was plummeting in a state of extreme joy. He paddled as he fell, but in reverse, and his mouth was wide. I watched him but he was lost in spray.

"That man looked familiar," I said to myself.

She overheard me. "Was he your brother or your uncle or your son? Perhaps he wrote the book you are reading?"

I shook my head. "This book was written a long time ago."

"A descendant of the author?"

"Highly unlikely but not impossible. Tell me something."

"Certainly, if I can..."

"What is so important about tea?"

"Nothing, nothing at all. It's the water that matters, the carrying of the water from the waterfall to the kettle. That's what I do when I am on a picnic. If there is no other source of water I will wait for the rain and catch it in my hands. I always let some or most of it go. Back into the wild."

Pisces

WE ARE ALL IN it together, like fish in the sea. We are all in the same boat. But make up your mind. Which is it? Are we fish or passengers? I don't see how we can be both, a boat full of fish isn't an image that inspires confidence, it seems to mean that we have been caught in nets and hauled to our deaths. I don't mind being in the same ocean as you, nor in the same boat, but we can't be in the same ocean and in the same boat at the same time. In the same boat and *on* the same ocean, yes, but that's quite different from what you are suggesting. On is not in.

Let's suppose that I am every man and you are every woman. After all, I am a man and you are a woman, and one man is very much like all men, and one woman is very much like all women. The differences are superficial. The qualities in common are far more important, that's what I believe anyway, and I suppose it is what all other men believe, because if I believe it they surely do too, for they are men and I'm a man. The same for you with women. This makes sense, doesn't it? If I am all men and you are all women, we can forget about being fish.

So we are in the same boat together, all of us, and because we are all men and all women, two boats are enough. I know I said we were in the same boat and yet we are on this lake in two separate craft but I can explain that away if you allow me. You are in your pedalo that is shaped like a fish, and I am in mine, also shaped like a fish, and chance has allowed our vessels to approach each other and now we are side by side, a pause in our afternoon, a chance to talk. We will pedal away in opposite directions in a few minutes, but that doesn't matter at all.

You see, the truth of the matter is that this lake is actually located on the deck of a massive ship. It's a pleasure cruiser of some sort and the facilities available are really very remarkable. One of them is a lake with little fish-shaped boats floating on it that passengers can use to pedal around for exercise, so we are all in the same boat but the truth of this is not immediately obvious. It appears that we are all in different boats, a dispersed flotilla of them, and that we are free to go wherever we please, that we are at liberty to ram and sink those other boats.

But that's just an illusion, I am afraid, though in fact I am not afraid at all, it's just a figure of speech and not a very good one. I am delighted that we are all in just one boat, the same boat, which happens to be so large we often forget about it, the same way we forget about the globe we live on, that the oceans rest on, that the cruise ship is sailing over. And now we have started drifting apart but that is unimportant. Even if I never see you again, it hardly matters. We are in the same boat, you and me, all of us, and there is nothing fishy about that fact.

Beyond Necessity

Kafka's Birthday

IT WAS FRANZ KAFKA's birthday. I baked a cake and wanted to take it to him but someone had clearly told lies to the person who drew the map I was using, because whenever I thought I was nearing my destination, I turned out to be mistaken. I was even further away than before. I kept trying to reach him but something always happened to prevent me from arriving. Eventually I managed to turn up at his house but his mother wouldn't let me through the door. I wanted to know if I would ever get to see Franz and she said, "Jetzt aber nicht," but I don't speak German and I couldn't reply, so I waited and waited. And waited. Finally I grew old and my strength failed me. By this time all the candles had burned out and the cake was very stale. Just before my death I asked his mother why no one else had ever come to wish Franz Kafka happy birthday and she leaned close and whispered, "Because this cake was meant only for you. Today is your birthday, not his." "But I don't like marzipan," I protested. "You've spoiled the parable now!" she growled.

One Mighty Bound

Suddenly, with one mighty bound, it was a dark and stormy night! A shot rang out. Life itself is a cliché. My pants are on fire. I hope the rain of this stormy night will put them out. The stormy night is no longer dark. The light from my burning pants illuminates the vicinity. Did I tell a lie? Is that why my pants are ablaze? Who fired the shot that rang out? Who set fire to my pants? There is an answer, bound to be one, a mighty bound.

Kissing With Noses

MOST PEOPLE KISS WITH lips, with tongues. But there are those who kiss with noses. It's not polite to stare at kissing couples but when you kiss with noses there is less to be seen. Lips must be puckered for a kiss but noses can remain as they are. A violent sneeze is a tenderly blown kiss to such people. I saw a man collapse in the street one day. His wife knelt by his side and gave him the kiss of life. But they were strangers to us and they were nose kissers and she simply rubbed her nose against his. Up he sprang, as good as new! And we, the nosey bystanders, sniffed in alarm at the strange sight and ran, like running noses on fevered faces.

Teachers

Teachers who say, "I teach Shakespeare," always astonish me for a few fraught moments before I suddenly realise that they mean they talk about the works of Shakespeare to a class of learners. In those few baffling moments I find myself wondering what exactly it is that they teach Shakespeare. Calculus? Geology? Ergonomics? And how and why and where?

In the Corner

He swallowed the morsels without savouring them. His stomach was so empty that he had to devour his hunger before he could eat his food. When he finished he tried to read a book. He saw the words but they could not see him. Then he decided to play the guitar. He sat on a stool in the corner of his room and plucked a chord. He had only one kind string on his guitar. The other five were nasty and mocked the melody like a peasant's sinews. They fought the notes like worms attacking eyeballs. He stood and walked to the mirror. And he wondered why mirrors reverse images horizontally but not vertically. He saw the room beyond the glass and it seemed a better place than the one he was in, though it was identical in shape and size. But the guitar in the corner had five kind strings and the books were full of words that could see him and the food tasted the way it should. And he yearned for that other world that was this world but not his world.

Fever

One of my friends had a fever but needed to go away on an important business trip. I offered to take the fever from him and look after it in bed for the duration of his trip. But I am a healthy individual and after a full night's sleep the fever broke. How will I be able to face my friend when he returns? I rush out to find a replacement fever but I can't locate one that matches it. I try gluing the broken fever back together but some of the pieces are missing. Maybe he will accept an injury in place of an illness? I wait patiently for him with my loaded shotgun.

Occam's Beard

Occam has stopped shaving. That's the news this morning. Does this mean we can now multiply entities beyond necessity? It's worth a try. I begin multiplying as many entities as I can and I keep multiplying them. Is it fun to do this or not? I can't decide. I ask my colleagues and they are also unsure. The entities object to being multiplied. They are different species, they say, but we continue to do what we have tasked ourselves with doing. The room is soon full of misshapen entities, monstrous hybrids, but we don't care. Occam is growing a beard. We keep multiplying them, driven by a mysterious impulse. It feels radical. There are so many entities in the room that they burst open the door and spill out into the world. Soon the entire surface of the planet will be packed with entities that have been multiplied beyond necessity. And as for ourselves? The sun has gone down, we are working late, we are tired. Let's call it a day and go home, wading our way through the brand new entities we have produced thanks to the miracle of multiplication. Our wives and girlfriends and husbands are slightly annoyed when we turn up. They ask, "Was any of this necessary?"

and we reply, "No, it is beyond necessity." And we wonder if we would look good with beards too.

Shadow Foot

SHE REMAINS THE ONLY person I ever saw trip over a shadow. I suppose other people have done the same thing but I haven't heard about them. I was sitting on a bench in the late afternoon sun, reading a book, and my shadow stretched out in front of me across the path, and along that path she came and she looked up at me, to see what was the title of my book, and her foot caught under my shadow and over she sprawled. I helped her to her feet. Actually I remained on the bench but my shadow hand reached out for her and she grasped it and I pulled her up. She was grateful but she wiped her fingers with a cloth that she extracted from the pocket of her trousers. The book was my autobiography and I am the only man in the world with a shadow that is exactly like treacle.

Baldness

BALDNESS IN MEN IS not natural but a result of civilisation. It probably comes from wearing tight hats or eating processed foods. In our original condition evolution would never choose baldness because the moonlight reflecting off the shiny scalp would give away our position to predators in the jungle. Men with thick heads of hair are less likely to be pounced on by tigers. They are more likely to be used as a paintbrush by gorillas, yes that's true, but pounced on by tigers, no! And yet, maybe we need more light at night. Could it be that bald men are necessary? The reflections of the male heads of an entire tribe might provide sufficient illumination for late sessions of applied mathematics to take place. Or for the continuance of guitar lessons.

Listening to Leonora

LISTENING TO LEONORA TELL a story is like opening an antique iron chest in which a thousand imps are babbling away simultaneously. Each imp has a different part of the tale to tell and the end result is like being struck repeatedly over the head with a grandfather clock. In a poor Leonora story the imps are both gagged and bound. In the tales I regard as average they are free to rant at leisure. But when Leonora is at her best, the imps are gagged but still allowed to convey meaning through darkly comic gestures. She is sitting in the conservatory at this moment and even at this distance I can clearly hear the swishing of those impish shrugs and the clicking of tiny twisted fingers. Follow me now and you will learn what is truly important. But mind your head on the clock.

The Contrast

I KEEP HEARING THE declaration that "you can't compare apples with oranges" but today I compared an apple with an orange by eating them both, and the orange won. It was slightly more delicious.

"No," cries an angry voice, "that's a contrast, not a comparison. You have drawn attention to the differences between them, not to the similarities. I ought to compare you with an apple. Let's see how you like it. You are both rotten to the core. I can't even tell you apart."

"Sorry, Father," I say, as I stand immobile in front of the tree. William Tell lifts his crossbow and takes aim. I hope he is joking and knows the difference between a boy and the apple on the boy's head. I will soon find out. But what a contrast between my life and the life of other boys my age!

The Leg Puppies

THE STRAY DOG MADE love to my leg. He came out of nowhere, began humping my shin. I tried to shake him off but it wasn't easy. Dogs do this and we wonder what is so alluring about our legs. The months passed and my leg swelled and I realised that it was pregnant. An unprecedented situation? I don't know. It's conceivable that other men's legs have been impregnated by hounds. I never heard of such a case, but I'd never heard of vulcanite saxophone cases before last year, so anything is possible. Not every man can know about every case in existence. In my final weeks I was confined to my bed. At last my leg burst open and the leg puppies came into the world. Each one was a miniature human leg with a little dog's head on the summit of the thigh. Before long they were hopping about and yapping. I made kennels for them out of crutches and old boots and now they all live with me and my leg has healed and I am a proud parent. They will inherit whatever legacy I can leave them, chiefly my thighbones and kneecaps.

When I Discovered Laziness

When I was young and full of energy, I read in a book that if every man, woman and child in China jumped up and down together, a tidal wave would be created by the vibrations that would engulf the United States of America. I remember thinking: so why don't they do that? If it's possible, why not make the attempt? Later, I read in a different book that every man, woman and child in the world could fit onto the island of Zanzibar, tightly packed together like skittles, and that the island would sink. Once again I asked myself: so why don't we do it? If it can be done, what's stopping us? Even later I was told by a teacher at my school that if every man, woman and child stood on the equator facing east in a line and took a step forwards, pushing back with their foot, the globe would stop spinning. So why aren't we lining up and stepping forward, I demanded to know? Many years passed before the answer occurred to me. Laziness! That is why there are no human-generated tidal waves, sinking islands or planetary brakes. Because people are too lazy to make them happen. It was the precise moment I discovered laziness and what it really means

and its importance to the daily workings and evolving history of
the human race.

Frankenstein Films

I WOULD LIKE TO see a new Frankenstein film made up of different parts from all the previous Frankenstein films. Such a film could be said, if you were in the mood to venture such a critical option, to be made in a form closer to the spirit of the original story. Sitting in the cinema, we would blink at the screen with our mismatched eyes, and outside later, while walking home, instead of a child, we would throw each other into the river.

The Giant Woman

THE GIANT WOMAN HAS kidnapped a gorilla, so they tell us, and is climbing one of the skyscrapers. She is almost at the top. They want us to take to the air and shoot her down. But we refuse. We loathe the idea of shooting a woman, even if she is a giantess, and we also worry about the gorilla. It is better to let events unfold without interference. We sip cups of tea in the hangar and our biplanes remain at rest. Later, one of us climbs onto the hangar roof with a pair of binoculars. He can see the city skyline clearly. The woman is perched on the summit of the skyscraper, blotting out many stars, but the gorilla is no longer in her grasp. Did she hurl it into the sky to create a new constellation in an effort to replace some of the stars stolen by her bulk? We are upset by this possibility. But no, the observer calls down to us with better news. He can see the gorilla now, asleep in a hammock woven from her long hair, a hammock stretched between her ears. We are happy again, full of tea and inaction, pilots at peace.

Exaggeration

I HAVE BEEN THINKING about exaggeration. People who refuse to exaggerate are implying that they only ever tell the truth about events, incidents and qualities. But perception is subjective and our evaluations are rarely accurate. We usually distort the details of things we try to remember. So it is impossible to tell the absolute truth about empirical phenomena. People who claim only to tell the truth can thus never tell the truth. Therefore people who don't exaggerate are liars. Therefore people who exaggerate are actually telling the truth. If I say I have two arms, I am telling the truth, thus I don't have two arms. If I say I have one hundred arms, I am exaggerating and exaggeration is truth, which means it is true that I have one hundred arms.

In the Den with Daniel

Daniel Day-Lewis is the best actor in the world. You know this. Everyone else knows this. Your wife knows it when you kiss her on the cheek before you set off for work. Your fellow commuters know it on the underground train that is always crowded at this time of the morning. Your colleagues in the office know it when you arrive. When you sit at your desk and switch on your computer you can't imagine how the simple truth could be different. He is the best actor in the world. There can be no argument.

He is more than an actor and this is why he is so magnificent. He inhabits his roles, he refuses to regard the characters he plays as separate from himself. He becomes those characters, absolutely without doubt or hesitation. He puts aside his own identity for the duration of the making of a film. He lives his role, no matter how uncomfortable, even when cameras aren't rolling. This is the supreme commitment to an art form and you admire him immensely. We all admire him. He is a marvel, a genius.

Whether he is playing a dramatic villain in remarkable circumstances or an ordinary man in an everyday situation, he is utterly convincing, not only to his fellow actors and the audiences of cinemas, but even to himself. When he plays a role, the role vanishes. The character is suddenly real, no less solid than I am. I am strolling the office floor today, chatting with the employees. I do this from time to time, to make them feel at ease. I approach your own desk. You swivel your chair and wait for me to speak.

"You have a wife, a child, a mortgage on a house. I have been asked by my superiors to make cuts to the workforce. I don't wish to do this. I know it will be difficult for any employee who is forced into redundancy. But I have my quota to fulfil. Jobs will be lost. You need to prove that you are invaluable. That is the only way you can secure your future here. Do you understand? Prove you are irreplaceable. Do this for me. Be irreplaceable, I am begging you. Please don't make it easy for me to dismiss you."

And you nod, but I see in your eyes that you have given up. At the end of the day, you rise from your desk to begin the journey home. You are descending the stairs and hear the words, "Finished," from above. Suddenly you remember that you are Daniel Day-Lewis, that your office job is fictional, the woman you call your wife is a fellow actor, your child doesn't exist. It was an act all along, brilliant, inspired, relentlessly perfect.

But you wonder. How can you be certain that Daniel Day-Lewis himself isn't just a character in another film?

Big Enough

WHEN A CRIMINAL GETS big enough he somehow becomes legitimate, untouched by the forces of law and order. While he is small-time, a petty miscreant, he is vulnerable to detection and arrest. But if he eludes capture long enough he will grow and there must come a point at which his status will change upwards with a single act. There will be one small theft that will propel the low criminal into higher non-criminal territory. This small theft is the golden key to his immunity. Do you see his hand reaching for the candy held by your child? If he succeeds in snatching the bar of chocolate, he will perform a quantum leap up the scale of criminality. He will turn into a kingpin and be safe forevermore.

The Skull

I KEEP A SKULL on a table at home. It is comforting to know it is there and that it won't run away on its own. In the past I made the mistake of keeping legs and arms instead. They always hopped or crawled away. I had no one to come back to in the evenings after work. But now I have a skull. I did manage to retain one hand by keeping it in a screw top jar. Have you ever tried to open a screw top jar with only one hand and from the inside? I thought not. It's impossible. I guess you are wondering what the skull does all day while I am working? It just so happens that I know the answer to that question. It thinks sweet, odd and tangential thoughts. How do I know this? Because it is my own skull. Yes, I go to work every day without a head. But I am an accountant, so nobody notices.

A Man on Stilts

THERE WAS A MAN on stilts and his stilts kept growing taller. He might have been an acrobat or fool, a visionary or scoundrel, nobody knew. At first he just stood on stilts that were as high as telegraph poles and he strode about the city with a perspiring face. But under the sheen of his sweat he was smiling. The following day his stilts had already doubled in height. And now he stepped over trams and trains with an ease that bordered on the obscene, as if the traffic was beneath his notice, as if those vehicles were discarded toys or slices of dropped cake. Within a week his stilts were so high he could step over any building in any city of the nation or indeed of any other country.

What can be said to such a man? How can anyone communicate with him? No crane could reach him, no ladder. A helicopter was sent up to negotiate, but the clatter of the rotors drowned out the conversation. An aeronaut in a balloon managed to float beside him for several hours. They discussed many topics but whether the exchange was cordial or heated is uncertain. A gust of wind puffed the aeronaut away over the ocean and he vanished. Long after we had given up hope of speaking with the man on stilts, of learning his name and intentions, a sheet of paper floated gently down to street level. It was a letter he had written to us. When we read it, we were compelled to grimace.

His handwriting was clear and his message unambiguous. His stilts would keep growing longer forever, he said. There was nothing we could do about the situation. There was nothing he could do. His destiny was an elevated one. Why fret about his altitude? Why worry about the ethics of his movements, the purity of his motives? Higher and higher he would go, his ersatz legs lengthening each day by a significant percentage. Soon enough, he would be able to stride from continent to continent. Then he would circumnavigate the globe in two or three quick steps. Finally he would be able to bridge the gap between this planet and the moon or even stand on other worlds.

We accepted this, some of us. Others argued for the cutting down of those monstrous stilts, for the burning of them, for the introduction of woodworm or woodpeckers. Anything to bring him back, to stop him striding about like the god of storks. We waited in vain for more letters to float down. At last it seems he rose up through the atmosphere until his head protruded beyond the bubble of air that permits life. His face was in space and he suffocated there. His body toppled and fell and burned up like a meteor. But a rumour began that he is still falling and this rumour has turned into a modern myth. People wait to be struck by his cadaver, to be grotesquely blessed.

The stilts themselves did not fall. They have grown so heavy that they are driving themselves slowly into the ground. They will push through the crust of our planet and ignite in the magma far below. In the meantime, we harness their sliding motion, connecting both stilts to a series of cogs and crankshafts, and we congratulate ourselves on our ingenuity. We might even find a practical use one day for the rotating toothed wheels. The letter from the sky has been obtained by the museum and it can be viewed in a glass case in one of the rooms, I have no idea which one. I never visit the museum. My grandmother is there, pickled in a jar, and I prefer to avoid gazing at her.

How Cold is It?

IT IS SO COLD that the candle flame just froze solid and I was able to snap it off and put it in my pocket for later. When it thaws out I will use it as a hand warmer and then put it back on the wick. In fact it is so cold that the flames of the fire have frozen solid and can be snapped off and used to cut butter, if cutting butter is something you need to do. It is so cold that the signs saying No Naked Flames near inflammable substances are unnecessary because the flames are all dressed in woollens. Yes, it is so cold that the sunbeams that came through my window froze into solid golden bars. And now the moon is shining through the window and the moonbeams are freezing into solid silver bars. The frozen sunbeams and frozen moonbeams have interlaced. It looks pretty but it means I am trapped in this chair until summer comes, if it ever does, and they evaporate.

Anatole France

I MET ANATOLE FRANCE one evening in a café in a nameless street. He was drinking absinthe and he turned to me when I entered. He said, "Listen to this. I once crossed Medusa with Thérèse Raquin and ended up with a very smelly cheese. Think about it. I mean, you don't have to think about it, if you don't want to, but if you do you'll get it."

"Gorgon Zola?" I replied, almost timidly.

He nodded his head and continued drinking. I didn't know what else to do, so I went over to an empty table in the far corner and avoided him for the remainder of the night. But as I was leaving, he leaned across and touched me. I looked down.

With his other hand he was offering something wrapped in a cloth. I took it and nodded my thanks. I walked home without examining it. At last I removed the cloth on my kitchen table.

My reflexes sometimes betray me, but on this occasion I discovered that the renowned man had given me a large lump of gorgonzola as a gift. His words echoed through my mind, "You'll get it."

I had got it. I never saw him again.

Anatole was a brilliant writer. But after his death it was discovered he had an extremely small brain. In fact it was so small that plans were drawn up to rename him Anatole Andorra or even Anatole Monaco. I know for sure these plans were never implemented.

The Birds

I SHAKE THE TREE and tiny absurd birds fly away. Later, at a reunion with my relatives, a giant hand shakes my family tree and all the aunts, uncles and cousins likewise scatter, me among them.

I extend my arms in order to glide safely and when my feet touch the ground and I recover my senses, the tiny absurd birds land on them and perch there, on both sides of my head. And here they are.

Postmodern Picnic

As Gregor Samsa woke one morning from uneasy metafictional dreams, he found himself transformed into a beetle. Not just any beetle but one with an air-cooled engine, the most famous Volkswagen car ever produced. For only a moment he was bewildered, then he turned his own ignition and trundled out of his driveway and down the cobbled street.

He had decided to make full use of his new automobile status. He went up the hill to the row of little cottages where his friend Franz lived, stopped outside and honked his horn. A curtain was pulled back in a tiny window and a troubled face peered out. "Hey, it's me!" cried Gregor. The window was thrown up. "But I don't know anyone called Herbie!" said the face. "I said Gregor, not Herbie! Are you deaf? You probably don't recognise me looking this way but I suppose that isn't a surprise. Nonetheless it is me."

Franz shut the window and a few seconds later he came out of the door and climbed into the car without saying another word. Nor did he fasten his seatbelt and in his mind he justified this decision by thinking how odd it would be for a passenger to do that with the driver's seat empty. Gregor revved his engine and they set off and left the city. There was clearly an unspoken agreement that they were going on a picnic, though they had no food.

But they couldn't find the picnic spot. Nowhere was a suitable place for a relaxing external meal and as for the precise location Gregor had in mind it just didn't seem to exist anymore, though Franz thought he glimpsed it once through a parting in the mist, far away. And they both grew old in the search and the food they didn't have went rotten and inedible. Finally it seemed that Gregor couldn't go another mile. "One last try!" urged Franz.

But it was useless. Gregor had broken down on the verge. At this point a policeman arrived on his motorbike. He tapped on the passenger window and Franz wound it down. Franz was now very old and his hearing was bad but it wasn't necessary for the policeman to shout to make himself heard. "The picnic spot is just a mile up this road. It was prepared especially for you and only you. I am now going to take away the grass and sky."

And Franz died. For the purposes of a proper ending.

The Leaves

You know how it is in autumn, when leaves swirl around our feet, wet leaves and crisp leaves. We always avoid the wet leaves, we know from experience how unsatisfying it is to kick them and step on them. They never fly very high and they certainly don't crunch pleasingly underfoot when they land. The disappointment is so strong that we feel sad for the remainder of the day. The colours of wet leaves might be enthralling, dark orange rimmed with red, light brown with yellow streaks. But colours aren't enough. This is a truth I learned from you when we first met in the ruins of the paint shop after the explosion. You declared that we were tins too, sloshing inside, tins with lids askew, but then you added that the comparison only applies to lonely individuals, and that lovers are more like leaves, fallen from the family tree, swirled together by the winds of time. I remember your words, partly because I fear them. But if we are leaves, are we not at the mercy of giants, beings from some other dimension who will delight in treading on us and crunching us melodically? I am a wet leaf, an insight accompanied by no feelings of shame, and so are you. We are too damp to be kicked high and crunched when we return to the ground. So who are the crisp leaves, the leaves the giants will go out of their way to step on? The answer is obvious to me. Knights in armour. No wonder there are so few knights in the modern world! The giants step on them through the autumns of history and flatten them into musical notes.

Stretching My Legs

I AM JUST GOING out to stretch my legs, I said, and I'll be back in one hour. Enjoy your walk, she replied, and that's exactly what I did. Along the vermilion beach I went, while the moon rose like an overripe peach. It cast my shadow onto the sands in a wonderfully elongated fashion. And then I knew that I was fated to arrive home early.

My wife was a trifle surly when I turned up. You only went out for twenty minutes and that's not one hour, she remarked. As I doubled up to enter through the door, I told her that I had stretched my legs most successfully in the lunar glow. With longer legs my stride was longer, my walking speed faster, and that explained my increased velocity.

I think you are positively absurd, she sneered. She was quite right, of course. And now my legs poke out of the bed at night and protrude out of the bedroom and slant down the stairs right to the bottom. They are the longest legs that any man has ever possessed. Oh, that trickster moon!

Do They Believe?

YOU BELIEVE IN GHOSTS. That's fine. But do ghosts believe in you? Just because a ghost claims to have seen you one night doesn't mean you are real. Maybe you are a figment of their imagination. I don't mean that you are a ghost to them in the same way that they are ghosts to you, that they exist and you exist but there is a misunderstanding about who is alive and who is dead. No, I wish to teach a darker truth. Ghosts don't exist. They are random sounds, the snapping of twigs in the dark forest, the wind in leaves, the splash of a nocturnal animal in a river. All natural effects that have been misinterpreted. And from the perspective of a ghost maybe that's what you are, a set of sounds that have no relation except in the mind of a ghost and now that ghost imagines your shape, your motivations, your history. But it is all an illusion. You never existed as an integral being and you never will exist. As you read these words try not to feel sad. Your misery is non-existent and useless, your self-pity wasteful.

The Mirror

I LOOK IN THE long mirror on the wall and make a strange face. My reflection makes the same face. I jump up and down and so does my reflection. I stand on one leg, shut one eye and blow a kiss. So does my reflection. My reflection is a copycat. It copies everything I do.

Wait a moment! My reflection is a flat surface, a vertical pool of photons and nothing else. It has no brain. It takes intelligence to mimic someone. If it doesn't have a brain how can it copy what I do? The only logical answer is that it isn't copying what I do. Therefore...

I must be the one who is copying it. I am the copycat!

My reflection laughs silently.

I laugh too, but I make a noise, the guffaw of despair.

The Underwater Trapeze

HAVE YOU SEEN THE underwater trapeze artist? She wears a diving suit and gently swings through the deeps beyond the coral reefs. The trapeze is attached to the bottom of the hull of a rusty ship and she requires no safety net if she loses her grip. Nets are, in fact, the enemy, for they might ensnare her as they drift on the unpredictable currents far below the surface, and her air would run out. Rogue nets, lost years ago by careless fishermen. On the high points of the arc of each swing, fore and aft, she enters that shimmering layer of the aquatic world where there is enough filtered sunlight to illuminate the tinted fish, but at the nadir of her sunken pendulum's path she is utterly and coldly, crushingly, shrouded by vast darkness, perennial and almost unknown. I saw her once only and I marvel still at her brass helmet as it glided in a symphony of bubbles past the porthole of my submarine like the egg of a drowned moon.

The Eleventh Commandment

THE ELEVENTH COMMANDMENT IS the only one nobody talks about. There are good reasons for our reticence. Firstly it was left behind on the mountain peak when Moses descended and there is a reluctance to humiliate that renowned figure by suggesting he made a mistake, that he was forgetful or physically incapable of carrying the extra tablet, which only had one commandment engraved on it. To climb down from a mountain carrying stone slabs is not an easy task even for a young man. We must bear the practicalities in mind. Secondly eleven is hardly an auspicious number. It seems superfluous, almost a joke. There is something pathetic about its appearance, two spindly legs without a body, a pair of eroded columns supporting the vanished roof of a doomed building. And what was the building used for? Perhaps it was a temple dedicated to a different god, which would explain the reluctance of Moses to bring it back or even to admit that it existed. Now the ruins are occupied by vagabonds and beasts. That is the truth of the number eleven. But the third reason is even more compelling. There was no need to bring that commandment down from the rocky heights. We already knew what it was. We were already living in absolute accord with its directive. Nothing can ever persuade us to break it. Thou shalt not understand. Of all the commandments it is the only one that everyone keeps.

The Façade

He is standing in front of the largest residential building ever constructed. The lights in all the windows of the apartments are burning. The façade is grand, a triumph of architecture, it resembles an antique computer. This is unusual and perhaps invigorating. But there is a storm, lightning forks across the night sky, thunder rumbles and the echoes bounce from the edifice, and he feels he is on the brink of a revelation. Then the lights go out. The façade is blank, a weight looming unseen in the darkness. After a moment, the lights come back on, but something has gone wrong, maybe the electromagnetism in the atmosphere has damaged the main control board that governs the illumination. The lights flash off and on again, and now the windows blaze in a rigorous sequence of sodium glows and impenetrable shadows. Every possible pattern that can be generated on a grid of almost a million rectangular pixels will appear over time, he knows this fact instinctively, the giant façade of the colossal building becomes a screen that depicts, in symbolic form, every visual potential, and thus every event that has ever happened, is happening and will ever happen, including the death of the observer, his own death. When this fateful image appears, he becomes a witness to the ultimate instant of his future, a future that is accelerating towards him. The observer sees himself sprawled before an immense building, a façade of windows, some lit and others in darkness, a grid depicting his own death. His representational self has collapsed from the stress of the immensity of the sight and its merciless implications. His heart has failed. The observer in the present also collapses when he sees this, from the stress of gazing on the sudden expiry of his symbolic heir, his avatar in lights. The present catches up with the future and they merge and he sinks to his knees, then topples forwards onto the chilly ground, while the sequence of flashing lights continues, foretelling every death, birth, story and dream that can be imagined.

The Ventriloquist

THE DOG TURNED TO look at me and it barked once. The man who held the lead jerked it in rebuke and the dog trotted after him. But I was unconvinced by the incident. The dog had barked without opening its mouth and the sound of the bark was somehow wrong. It did not match the expression in the dog's eyes. I wondered if its owner was a ventriloquist. He probably played this trick several times a day. I was right about this but I was unable to prove it. I never saw the man or the dog again. I only heard rumours about him. As it happened, he eventually admitted the deceit to his closest friends. His dog was always silent and he was the one who barked. They said to him, "If you can imitate the bark of a dog so well, why not speak human words on the dog's behalf?" They thought it would be even more amusing if the dog looked at a person and said, "How are you?" in a polite voice. Pretending to bark was only half a joke and unworthy of the ventriloquist's talents. But the ventriloquist explained that this suggestion was beyond his abilities. He could not speak any human words. The friends were shocked when they understood that he had indeed never spoken to them. He had made himself understood in other ways. He left them and went home. Once inside his house he deflated in a corner and the dog jumped onto the sofa and yawned. The man could bark but not talk for the simple reason that the dog was the ventriloquist and the man was the puppet. I turn to look at every dog I pass in the street now and we exchange knowing glances.

The Gorgon

Medusa has snakes for hair, but what of that? Her glance can turn you to stone, but why be angry at the thought? Don't you realise that she herself has fears of her own, namely that she will meet a demon with mongooses for hair and eyes that can turn stone into flesh. Every monster has its opposite. A hero once tried to kill her, long before Perseus managed to do so, and this hero entered the temple in which she lived and her snakes hissed a warning. She woke, raised her eyelids and petrified him. When that reverse gorgon enters the temple, the hero will be made into a man again, but that is not Medusa's main worry. The temple around him will also turn into living flesh. Then the hero will drop his sword and run for a comforting hug to the gorgon. They will clutch each other tightly, both of them with eyes shut, as the building, which has transformed into the stomach of an unknown god, begins to digest them.

The Fireman

His name was Terence and he had been brought up to be careful when using water. He would bathe in a cupful of water and use only a thimbleful to wash the dishes after dinner. He was told it was a sin to allow water to escape down the plug hole. When he grew up he became a fireman. Now he points a hose at a burning building and directs a jet of water onto the flames, but only for a few seconds, until the steam obscures his vision. Now he shuts off the valve, lays the hose on the ground and hurries to collect the steam in a large bag so it can be recycled. Terence is a conscientious citizen but not a good fireman.

Infinity Gears

THERE WAS A FELLOW who invented a machine with many gears. The machine consisted of almost nothing but gears, in fact. Gears were the point of the device. It had a frame and a handle but its most remarkable feature was a meshed collection of one hundred thousand gears. I think that was the number. But anyway, if you turned the handle the first cog would rotate. You had to turn it ten times to make the second cog turn just once. Then the second had to turn ten times to make the third cog turn once. The third cog had to turn ten times to make the fourth turn once. And so on.

I am sure you can picture the contraption. The final gear inside the device would turn so slowly that it would take until the end of time before it made even a single revolution. What I mean is that the universe would have ceased to exist before that ever happened. But you know something? The inventor wasn't really interested in making a point about time. His plan was to operate the machine in reverse, to forcibly turn the last gear once so that the whole causal chain of cogs would accelerate to ludicrous speeds, each cog spinning ten times faster than the preceding one. Do the calculations!

That's correct. The first cog would end up spinning as fast as the speed of light, which should be impossible, because it has some mass. So its mass would increase in accordance with the Laws of Relativity and it would rapidly acquire infinite mass as a consequence. What does this mean? It would turn into a black hole. The Earth would be torn apart by the black hole. Yes, he was so bitter that he wanted to destroy his own planet and annihilate all life upon it, himself also. He turned the last cog once and laughed as he did so. This was his revenge upon the miseries of his resented existence.

He had to apply a lot of force to make that final cog turn. He managed to do this and the next cog in the sequence turned faster, the next one even faster and so on, but only a hundred cogs later the sequence came to a spectacular halt. His scheme was defeated. A few cogs around the hundred mark were spinning so fast they vaporised from the heat generated and the inventor was killed by the scalding metallic gas that suddenly filled the room. The machine was broken now and the Earth was saved. But nobody else was ever aware that the planet had been threatened in such a manner.

Walking the Wrong Plank

THERE IS A WISE old saying that I think comes from China. *The twisted tree lives its full life, while the straight tree ends up in planks.* But nobody told Captain Worst about this. He anchored near an island one day and told his men to row ashore and cut down a tree to make planks. The island was tiny and only one tree grew upon it and that tree was the most twisted tree imaginable. I suppose the wind had knotted it while it was growing. Now it was mature, an astonishing tangle of loops, but the men had their orders and they cut it down and made planks from it. Captain Worst was annoyed but what could he do? A pirate must follow certain customs. He wanted his captives to walk the plank and the straighter planks of his ship could hardly be used for that purpose. He was against leaks just as much as he was against leniency. The twisted planks would have to suffice and satisfy.

I once had occasion to try out one of these planks. Prodded on the point of a cutlass I took a first step on my final walk. The other steps followed. The first part of the plank jutted out over the ocean in the way a pirate's plank should, but soon it curled around and looped up and back. I had to crawl to keep my balance, grip the sides with my fingers, take deep breaths to settle the dizziness in my head. A spiral, a helix, dipping, rising, twisting, and suddenly I was above the deck of the ship once more. I dropped down behind Captain Worst. It took only a little nudge to propel him over the side. Now I am in charge, as tradition dictates, and I am better than he was, a little better. I am Captain Better and I pay heed to wise old sayings.

The Sea and the Ruins

WHEN I REACH THE sea, after trekking over the dunes, I kneel and insert the straw that I have been carrying into my mouth and then I drink the sea, all of it, with a tremendous slurping noise. This is my function. The king of the gods ordered me to do it, I can't remember if it was Zeus or Odin or someone else, so much time has passed. But I drank and drank and eventually the ruins of Atlantis were exposed. In which case, I suppose it was Zeus. The broken buildings look quite different from the way they have been imagined ever since the continent sank. Soon the birds and monkeys will come and take the place of the departing fish. Is that an improvement? It is not for me to say. Nothing is for me to say because I must keep my mouth clamped shut. If I open it even a tiny fraction, the water inside me, which is under phenomenal pressure, will jet out with such force that it will cut through solid rock. And then the ruins will be even more ruined. And that is not the correct way to ruin ruins. The only correct way to ruin ruins is to use the rubble to construct elegant new buildings.

Inside the Minotaur

When Theseus kills the Minotaur he stabs the beast in the heart and then pulls out his sword and slices across the lower abdomen. It is essential to ensure the monster is humiliated as well as killed. But as the innards fall onto the floor of the stone chamber Theseus sees that they do not loop like those of a man. The guts form the outline of a maze, the very labyrinth in which they are standing, and in the centre is a tiny model of the Minotaur. We can suppose that within this miniature replica there are yet more guts that form a maze and a smaller model trapped inside them. Theseus still holds with his free hand the cord that Ariadne gave him to guide him back out, but he no longer needs it. Here is a map of the route written in flesh and he will follow it like a morsel of digested food and it is he, not the beast, who will feel degraded.

The Prison

Observe the layout of the prison and please understand that it is constructed like a maze not in order to make escape more difficult but to obstruct entry.

A thief is caught and sentenced to five years in jail. He is escorted by guards to the gate of the building. That gate is opened. Now the guards become guides, they must lead him to his cell. But how can they find it?

They climb a few flights of stone stairs, turn a few corners and walk along half a dozen corridors, but they soon grow reluctant to venture too deeply into the maze, for they fear they might be stuck inside forever. Thus they make only a token effort at finding his cell. The prisoner follows slowly, dragging his feet, aware that the entire process is just a charade.

The guards decide to stop, turn around and retrace their steps. Eventually they are at the gate again, heaving sighs of relief. Later they will write a report together on old yellow paper and mail it to their superior officer. They looked for the cell but it has gone missing. The prisoner has been returned to freedom because they have nowhere else to put him.

The superior officer, an experienced sergeant, reads the report and nods in approval. One day, the correct cell will be located and the prisoner will be shut inside, and the situation will become more dangerous for the warders, who will have to risk getting lost every time they deliver a meal to the felon. It is safer when the guards write and send a report like this one.

In this enormous building there is only one true prisoner, a trespasser who entered through the roof weeks ago and found himself in sole possession of the empty spaces within. He was sentenced to one month in absentia when his case came to light. With luck, after he has served his sentence, in another week or so, he will find his own way out, a reverse trespass on the even larger and far more labyrinthine territory of the outside world.

Head in Hands

THE MAN IS HOLDING his head in his hands. Last year he played football with it. The year before that, he rolled it down a mountain slope just to see how fast it could go. The year before that, he took it off and put it on backwards, so that he could see where he had been while leaving it a mystery where he was going. The year before that, he extracted all the awareness of time from his brain, or maybe it wasn't that particular year. Who knows? There are worse things he could hold in his hands in public. Let's not judge him too harshly. Let us not act like those other things we are grateful he is not holding.

The Windmill

A WINDMILL STANDS ALONE on the heath. The ponderous sails turn anticlockwise. Despair finds me here, also alone, after creeping up, eyes glinting through the dirty windows, a footfall creaking in my bones as I cast the grapple upwards. The barbs snag on a sail and the wire is pulled taut and the noose around my neck tightens. Then I am lifted off the ground and the wire sings a carefully chosen note, the first of a melody that will never be composed. The sun rises and mud wasps drone in the cool of my shadow. I wait for the ancient knight on the thin horse to arrive and battle my giant gesture. But I am dead already and turning blue as I turn endlessly on this rotary washing line. If you see him passing on the road, tell him that there is no need to hurry.

Alexander Kluge

I WAS AT THE opera with Alexander Kluge. It's strange, I know he loves opera, but every night this week he has been there, and I have been there too. A disturbing coincidence. His eyes met mine. My eyes met his. I was embarrassed, I looked down, I don't know whether he looked down too but I think he probably did. On the other hand, I remember one of his most famous quotes, "I've always wanted to see what my head looks like from above," and I am increasingly doubtful that he has ever lowered his gaze in the traditional manner. What should I do? Every night this week, I'm not joking, the same opera. I wanted to leave the last time I saw him, but it would have created a scene.

The really odd thing is that he approached me after the show. He must have loitered beyond the final crescendo, waiting for the other members of the public to vacate the building. How he found me so easily is still unclear. Does he own a map of the building? He didn't introduce himself, but I knew who he was, and his anxious expression and bulging eyes made the situation even more awkward because part of me wanted to tell him how much I loved his films, especially *Der große Verhau*, and his books, including *Das Labyrinth der zärtlichen Kraft*, but I wanted him to speak first. That was unwise.

I thought perhaps he was going to apologise for unnerving me, for making me feel he was a spy, that I was being monitored, analysed, threatened in some intangible way, but to my astonishment he accused *me* of stalking *him*. And he demanded an explanation. Why was I present at the opera whenever he was? It wasn't acceptable behaviour on my part, it was possibly pathological, what kind of strange agenda did I have? He had been on the verge of leaving his seat and making himself scarce, but it was against his principles to flee from threats, and maybe he ought to have assaulted me instead.

When he paused to take a breath, I blurted, "But I am an opera singer, the main star, the renowned baritone, and I have agreed to appear on the same stage every night and sing the same arias. I signed a contract. That's why I am there every night. I am compelled by the terms of my profession, and it's not fair that you should attend every performance and blame me for it. I do the best I can. I wish our roles were reversed and you were on stage in a cumbersome costume while I was sitting comfortably in a chair as part of the audience. Those are the facts and pardon me for stating them so bluntly."

Washing Our Hands

We wash our hands very thoroughly. That is the custom in our land. We take them off one at a time and drop them in a bucket of soapy water. Then we stand in the bucket and churn the suds into eruptions of dirty froth with our feet. When we are finished, we kick the bucket over to drain it. Returning our hands to our wrists is the tricky part. It is said that in olden days there was a simpler way of washing our hands, but the method was never written down and no one knows how it worked. Washing machines are gradually being introduced to our towns. Soon we will perch on stools and watch our hands spin around behind the glass of the portholes. But is this really progress? When we wash our hands in buckets our feet are washed at the same time. Now we must find a way of removing our feet so they can revolve inside the machines too. I twist my foot to work it loose but the bones are jammed. Many things in this world are clean but none are easy.

How to Wake Up

Before my first cup of coffee I am never fully awake. I can understand how this might also be true for others. I work from home and I have always felt annoyed that my computer runs slow in the mornings. A quirk of the power supply or an inscrutable software problem? I had no idea. Then by accident I knocked over a cup and the strong coffee inside poured into the keyboard, soaking the circuits beneath. Aha! Suddenly the computer began working at high speed. It was truly awake for the first time in its existence. Why had it never occurred to me that it might need coffee just as urgently as I do? Since that moment I have been alert to the requirements of inanimate objects around my home. I even know that my cup of coffee needs a cup of coffee to wake itself up. I always prepare two cups as soon as I leave my bed. The first cup is drunk by the second cup, then I drink the second cup, the cup that is now fully alert. Listen to me, my sleepy friends! There is no better way than this to wake up.

The Umbrella

"I CARRY AN UMBRELLA to protect my head from rain," says the old woman while standing next to her grandson on the intriguing landscape. "But it hasn't rained for many days and probably won't today," he replies.

"You misunderstand me, perhaps because you are young," she says with a gentle smile, and she points at the scene before them. There are fortified walls that climb the slopes of hills and the entire region has a mythic magic about it, one that is both delicate and rugged, and this combination gives the vista a flavour unique in the age in which they dwell.

"To protect my head from reign, not from rain," she explains.

"What does that mean?" he asks.

"The reign of a king, of tyrants. They were abolished when I was little, just your own age, but I always worry they might return one day. And that is why I carry this umbrella. If they come back, they will occupy these fortifications and establish a base for themselves from which they can oppress the people. Do you understand now? It's all very logical."

"How can an umbrella protect you from kings?"

"Because of the way it's made."

He says nothing, merely waits for an explanation, and she finally stoops to tell him in a low voice, "The canopy is the skin of a large phoenix. Allow me to demonstrate on that tower over there."

She closes the umbrella, points it like a musket, presses a hidden trigger on the handle and a bolt of flame erupts from the tip, the ferrule, and widens as it screeches across the distance. It strikes the tower and explodes, bringing down the structure with a crash of blocks.

The canopy has vanished and the old woman is left holding nothing but a stick with bare wires at the end.

"But now you have wasted the shot," he says.

"No, for it's a phoenix."

And even as he watches, the canopy regrows and once again the umbrella is whole. She opens it and holds it above her head and together they watch as the overheated stones burst like bubbles.

Song of the Sirens

ODYSSEUS REMAINS THE ONLY mortal man who heard the song of the Sirens and lived to tell the tale. But he never actually told the tale. He was very reluctant to talk about his experience. Only once, when drunk on resinated wine, did he dare reveal what he thought of the resonance of those mythical voices. His wife sat quietly in the corner, knitting an amphora, while he slurred his words. First he mentioned how his crew's ears had been plugged with wax, then he went on to detail his binding to the mast of his ship, the type of strong rope his men used to safely secure him so he wouldn't go mad and throw himself overboard and drown as he struggled to swim to those magnificent but malevolent maidens on their rocks. He heard the song as they sailed past but he was disappointed in the music. And when his wife gently asked what they sounded like, those three weirdly beautiful singers, Odysseus took another gulp of wine and said, "One was like a police car, another like an ambulance, the third like a fire engine," and he sighed and poured himself more wine but the vessel was empty. "Do you really think it's a good idea to knit amphorae?" he asked her. "The wine keeps leaking out." Then he rested his head on the table among the olives and slept.

The Slipper Exchange

SHE WENT TO HER sister's house to exchange a pair of slippers for two bananas. Then she understood that she had in fact exchanged ordinary slippers for special ones. She peeled the bananas and ate them. Then she tied the skins around her feet. When we step on a banana skin, we slide and fall. But if the skins are part of us we can glide along happily. She skated home in her new footwear, yellow with brown freckles, and because she lived fairly close to her sister she took the long way back, along busy streets and through the market. The vegetable vendors applauded as she weaved effortlessly between the stalls. Only once was she overtaken, by a man on a bicycle with watermelons for wheels. In the meantime her sister sat in an armchair, peeled one of the slippers and ate it. Then she peeled and ate the other slipper. The discarded skins lay on the floor and dreamed of a better world shaped like a footstool.

The Palace

"WAR IS COMING! PESTILENCE and famine! There will be misery and chaos across the world! Out of my way..." cried the Lord as he spurred his horse to a gallop through the narrow streets of the town.

It was a small town, not much bigger than a village really, and Myron was returning from the well with a bucket of water. The bucket was balanced on his left shoulder and blocked his sight in that direction. He began to cross the street and then heard the thunderous hooves.

"Move aside, you fool!"

The Lord refused to slow his steed but lifted the hand that gripped his whip and lashed out at Myron. The tip of the whip cracked against the wooden side of the bucket and toppled it over, almost.

Half the contents were spilled, but not all, and the water soaked Myron on one side only. Then the Lord had raced past him and the wind of his rush made the ends of Myron's shirt flutter.

The Lord galloped off and Myron saw him become a tiny figure kicking up dust on the road that curved away from the town towards the palace, that vast edifice of big stones, protected by an astoundingly high wall, a drawbridge over a fathomless chasm, more than one portcullis, and ponderous doors of brass that were festooned with barbed spikes.

The palace was a fortress, imposing, secure, a refuge from the despair and desperation of the outer world. It was a sanctuary for the Lord and would be his place of voluntary confinement until the coming catastrophe was over, however long it lasted. Myron sighed deeply.

He watched the Lord cross the drawbridge. The first portcullis opened to admit him, then the second, then the third, and closed behind him. After that, he was lost to sight, but the clang of the ponderous doors faintly reached Myron's ears, a grim sound, rather sad too.

Then the drawbridge was raised and locked in chains. The palace had gone into hibernation. Or rather, it had sealed itself from the dangers of reality and set sail into the future but without moving. It was a static ark. No doubt it was filled with enough supplies to last years.

Myron adjusted the position of the depleted bucket on his shoulder, sighed again, and resumed walking. He returned to his tavern, entered through the back entrance and delivered the bucket to the kitchen. The cook was preparing some simple meals from the few vegetables available. Myron passed through an inner door and emerged in a drinking room.

"The Lord has finally come back," he said quietly.

He waited for the reaction.

The handful of customers looked up, licking their lips, some shaking their heads, whether in wonderment or doubt was difficult to say. Myron took a glass and pulled himself a frothing beer.

"He has sealed himself into the palace. Because of the coming war and the devastation that will follow," he added, then he took a valiant gulp, draining the glass in one convulsive action.

"Leaving us in the lurch," was his next comment.

The customers grumbled.

He addressed them as if he was a professional teller of tales, a raconteur or troubadour. "Safe up there in his gilded coffin, the seasons will be unseen and unfelt by him. They will pass and he will grow weaker, in mind as well as body, turning into a bloated degenerate, a grotesque parody of himself, a figure ruined by overindulgence and inactivity, rendered superfluous to history by an overrich and meaningless existence."

Pouring himself another beer, Myron continued, "Eventually he will say to himself 'The war must be long over now, the pestilence gone, the famine an event belonging only to the past. It is time to order the spiked doors opened, to raise every portcullis and lower the drawbridge, to set forth again and reclaim my realms, to resume my glorious rule.' And so he will emerge into the light, a blinking toad, pallid and gross."

Myron consumed this second beer more cautiously. "He will learn that he has made a grave error. There was no war, pestilence did not come, famine was avoided, the land was at peace. He had hidden away for nothing. His predictions were wrong, all of them. Half a century passed and he wasted it. Down into the town he totters, for he has forgotten how to ride, and no one he meets is able to remember him. He is unrecognised."

Spreading his arms wide, Myron cried, "When he demands respect, he is mocked. When he ineffectually loses his temper, he is laughed at. He collapses into the mud of the street and nobody comes to help him up. His reign is over, of course, but worse than that for him. It is as if he never ruled at all. And I will stand in my tavern, just as I am doing now, and tell you his story, and you won't know whether to believe it or not."

One of the drinkers was gazing through the window. He frowned, pointed a gnarled finger into the distance.

"The drawbridge is coming down," he said.

There was murmuring.

Myron hurried to the window to peer out. "But the palace has been shut for fifty years. What a time for the Lord to emerge! Just when I was telling you the story about how he almost rode me down. So long ago. He lashed out at me, his whip struck my bucket, I spilled water down my side." He stared at his left leg, as if to confirm it was dry. "I wanted to tell you what happened on that day. First I went into the kitchen, then I came into this room and began my story. I wonder what the Lord looks like now?"

One of the customers turned to Myron.

"Who?" he asked.

"The Lord. The former ruler of this realm," said Myron, squinting. Even at this distance he could tell that the figure emerging from the palace was feeble, a physically weak specimen, a dodderer.

"We were ruled?"

There was astonishment in the speaker's tone.

"Once, long ago..."

Myron turned away from the window. He was a very old man now but still reliable on his feet, still strong. But he wondered if he had lost the ability to tell tales convincingly. The technique he had always relied upon to generate surprise and drama seemed to have let him down. Mixing up the past and present tenses. It had worked well before today.

"He is approaching the tavern," said the drinker at the window. "Whoever he might be, he is coming here."

Myron considered this turn of events and shrugged. Then he had an idea. A withered old whip hung on a nail in the wall above the fireplace. Just one of the ugly ornaments the tavern boasted. There were pewter mugs, cracked plates, the dented helm of a defeated knight, a rotten blunderbuss, an oil painting so grimy it was impossible to say what it depicted, and this whip. It was stiff with age and creaked as Myron painfully took it down and straightened it. He cracked it once to take out the rigidity. The leg of a stool broke off and was flung into the corner with a rattle like desecrated bones.

Turning to face the door, Myron waited.

Pressed Flowers

HE WAS READING AN illustrated book about flowers and someone had pressed real flowers between the pages. It was a massive book, a volume he had brought down from the attic with a pulley and ropes. It belonged to the former owner of the house. Now it rested flat on the dinner table. Each page was bigger than he was and turning them was like lifting the lid of an ancient sarcophagus to reveal an unknown and unusual pharaoh. The dried flowers had no more scent than the paintings that represented them and the colours had faded, but something about the act of preserving them touched him. He was also amused. Then he turned another page and saw there was no pressed flower. What had happened? He leaned forward into the book as if searching for grains of pollen. His wife chose this very moment to enter the room. The opening of the door startled him and he fell forward into the book. The extra weight caused the table to collapse and the book slammed shut with him inside it. He too was a pressed flower. Like a bookmark he would keep the page of his fate. His wife stooped to pick up the book and with no discernible effort found a place on the widest and deepest shelf for it.

The Octopus and the Clock

I WATCHED AN OCTOPUS wrestle with a clock under the sea. Occasionally the strange pair would rise to the surface, tentacles and pendulum striking blows against each other. The octopus was attempting to turn back the hour and minute hands, but it was impossible for me to know why. The clock was large with a case made of thick hardwood. It must have fallen off a ship in the middle of the night. I stood upright in the skiff with my harpoon poised but the target was moving too erratically. I might hit the octopus by mistake. At last they sank out of sight in the turbulent waters and vanished for good. But is it really so good? I lower my harpoon and sigh. Time always eludes me at the last moment but why? Because the last moment and all other moments belong wholly to it.

My Swiss Neighbour

MY NEIGHBOUR STANDS IN his garden, a man with no limbs and no head. I observe him over the fence as one arm emerges from his hollow body, then another, then a third, all of different lengths. He has multiple legs too. All these limbs serve a different function, some are serrated, others can grasp objects like tweezers. Occasionally he will stick his head out like a cautious tortoise and it can be seen that he has a face exactly like a magnifying glass. What does his wife think of his abilities? Does she enjoy extensions that he never reveals in public? He is a versatile and durable man. Only his corkscrew arm is a little bent out of shape. He damaged it on his own wedding champagne, he tells me, a jeroboam. We all have minor injuries of that sort, I reply. It begins to rain, the conversation is over. He retracts all his extensions and his wife comes out with a wheelbarrow to take him back inside. None of his arms includes an umbrella, an oversight. I return into my own house and find myself questioning my own utility.

The Palace Coup

Let me tell you what political life is like in the Kingdom of Vestibule. The system of government there is rather unusual. It is an absolute monarchy and individuals are picked by lottery to be king. Only males are eligible. This is because the outdated computers responsible for running the lottery are damaged beyond repair and incapable of understanding societal equities. The kingdom is an atavistic one in other respects too.

The chosen citizen is removed from his ordinary dwelling and taken to the palace, where for the next six months he learns his royal duties. While living in the palace, he struggles to remember what his predecessors were like. Did he, in fact, have any predecessors? Might he actually be the first king of his nation? If so, what was Vestibule before he ascended the throne? A republic? These are questions his retainers refuse to answer. He concludes it is beneath his dignity to persist with his historical inquiries.

But one morning, his most senior advisor visits him while he is still at rest in his enormous royal bed. The advisor leans over him and whispers into his ear that the moment he was chosen by the lottery the process spontaneously created an assassin whose task is to overthrow him. This is the nature of the procedure, a physical law. The moment anything appears, its opposite must also come into being. A ruler must have an assassin.

"I am astonished to hear this," confides the king.

The advisor shrugs.

"But I will heed your warning, of course," adds the king, and then wants to know how likely the assassin is to succeed. The advisor grins and insists that the king has nothing to worry about.

"The palace is secure and the guards are highly trained and fiercely loyal. I think you can disregard the danger."

The king is reassured and begins to enjoy his reign. He visits the various cities, towns and villages of Vestibule, sails to other continents, waves at everyone from a distance, always surrounded by guards. But gradually the pleasures of privilege decay back into anxieties and an inexplicable mood infects him.

He feels that something is not quite right.

Once again he asks his chief advisor about the fabled assassin and this time there is a significant pause before he receives the reply, "The likelihood of him ending your life is low but not zero."

This is less reassuring than the previous analysis of the assassin's chances and the king is displeased. He makes his annoyance known to the advisor, who once again merely shrugs. The king's reign continues but it is like a foot with a thorn in the sole, moving forward always in discomfort. For the king, the pain is the awareness of a threat lurking in his periphery. He periodically asks about the assassin and his advisor answers him.

"The assassin is very cunning and his plans for your termination are surely worrying. I will double the guard..."

Each time the king enquires about the assassin, the reassurance he receives from his advisor is less potent. Finally he understands that assassination is highly probable. He decides to accept the inevitable. He summons the advisor to his throne one evening and demands:

"How will the assassin accomplish my overthrow? This is the question that concerns me more than any other."

"I don't know the precise method."

"Do you have any information you can share with me?"

"Only generalities."

The king nods. "Let me hear them."

The advisor strokes his long beard and says, "The truth of the matter is that he will destroy you not only in space, but also in time: not only in what is called the present, preventing you from having a future, but in the past too. You will be totally obliterated, so thoroughly it will be exactly as if you had never existed. That is the great mystery of this special assassin. That is his terrible genius. You will be utterly cancelled out."

The king feels cold droplets of perspiration trickle down his brow. But with a monumental effort, he controls himself. He asks, in a firm but polite voice, his eyes unblinking, how his predecessors, the former kings, coped with this threat. How did they manage the assassin?

He is met with a blank stare. "Former kings?"

This is too much. He stands and casts off his cloak. Then he clenches a fist and shakes it in the face of his advisor.

"Those who won the lottery before me! Who else do you suppose I mean? I demand to know what evasive action they took. They certainly must have done something to defend themselves!"

The advisor is genuinely bewildered.

"Won the lottery before you? But you are the first winner. Former kings? What former kings? You are the first king. Vestibule was always a republic before now. The computers decided to change the system. I was against it but I am only a servant. It was a republic."

And with a frown he mutters, "Wasn't it?"

Whirlwind Romance

I don't know how they met but it wasn't long before they were completely in love and spinning around together like a gyroscope of glee. There was so much passion that it resulted in a circular motion that accelerated daily. It became a hazard in public places, this vortex of desire, a rotating couple, flesh joined as one, knocking down other pedestrians like skittles, sucking up and flinging away all lost objects, bursting apart the tables and chairs of outdoor cafés, the pair oblivious inside their shield of centrifugal kisses, carried away. A whirlwind romance is a natural disaster and the deeper they are in love the faster it spins. I feared the city might be destroyed. Lost in each other, they nonetheless toyed with the destinies of many innocent unloved lives. They had to be stopped. We cast nets over them, but the force of the whirl shredded them into ribbons. We flung harpoons that were deflected by the impenetrable twist and I hurt my wrist doing so. Jets of cold water from hoses were turned into hot vapour as soon as they connected with the rim of the spin. We were at a loss. Then a voice shouted out, "Tornado," and we stood back to watch.

They were spinning one way, the tornado another, and at precisely the same speed. The tornado bounced between the houses in the narrow streets and found its way into the central square of our metropolis like a drunken acrobat. It lurched around the public space and if it owned a face I would have discerned an expression of amusement there, but tinged with a deeper and older melancholy. It had already snatched laundry off washing lines and now it was drying underwear as an unconscious favour, but when by pure chance it connected with the whirlwind of the passionate couple the clothes were all ejected at once. The two equal but opposite vortices cancelled each other out. They both remained static in time and space. But all that kinetic energy had to go somewhere, and it was transferred to the city itself, which began spinning, first one way, then another, making us giddy, turning us into dancers and romancers. We still seek answers but they will have to wait.

The Witch

THE WITCH LIVES IN a cave that is dominated by a cauldron. The liquid is seething inside this immense iron pot. The witch stirs the mixture with a wooden spoon as long as she is tall. Bubbles break the surface of the brew and float high, then burst, releasing a foul steam that has traces of sweetness in it. The cave is soon foggy with the vapours of the potion. The full moon shines through the opening of the cave, the heavy beams turning the steam a sickly yellow hue. What spell is the witch casting? This is the beauty of the occult chemistry at work here. The spell can be for anything. The evil drink is made, then consumed, and the witch will have the power to perform one extraordinary act. She can choose to levitate or breathe underwater, to pass through walls like a ghost or make her skin proof against bullets and pitchforks. She can become flame-resistant, immense or tiny, can transform into an animal or a hybrid made of many beasts. She can stretch her legs to an incredible length, enabling her to stride many leagues in minutes or hop over chasms. She can amplify the sensitivity of her eyes or ears.

She can grow an extra head with another brain, two extra heads even, doubling, tripling her already considerable intelligence.

The potion is ready at last. And so she discards the long wooden spoon like a warrior casting aside a broken lance. Then she picks up a ladle and dips it into the brew, raises it to her gnarled lips. She sucks the fluid into her mouth, squints at the taste, grimaces but swallows, her throat pulsing and burning. The ladle is drained, she dips it again. She is required to drink the entire contents of the iron cauldron before the power will come to her. It is not an easy task. But she has an inhuman determination, she is possessed of incredible stamina. She empties the second ladle, dips a third time, drinks that one too, then a fourth, a fifth, a sixth. Her stomach swells alarmingly but this is a supernatural concoction, it won't fill her to the point of bursting. It will turn into dark energy as she digests it and her stomach will return to its normal size.

At last the metal of the ladle scrapes against the base of the pot, scooping a few remaining puddles of brew. She consumes these with relief. The cauldron is empty. Or rather, there is no more liquid inside it, but a thick crust of burned and stinking purple residue coats the bottom and sides of the vessel. This concretion, fused together in extremely dense layers, also stains the ladle, entombing it like an effigy smothered in plaster. In fact the cauldron has spat clumps of the potion onto the walls and floor of the cave. Her home is a mess. She sighs as she gazes at the smears and blotches, the splashes and smudges, the ugly blemishes of the malignant elixir's making. It will be so difficult and time-consuming to clean up the pollution, to scrub the utensils, the cave itself, a chore almost beyond all her reserves of physical strength. She grins sourly as she understands an ironic truth that generations of witches have learned before her. She brims with dark energy and is able to cast a single spell. What shall it be? To turn into an eagle or mole? To charm the heroes of the land outside to fall in love with her? To soar upwards and visit other planets? To be immortal?

There is only one spell she can possibly consider casting now. Every atom of her being compels her to follow this course of action. Raising her arms high, chanting the words of mystic power, she orders the cauldron, the ladle, the walls and the floor to clean themselves, to scrub themselves until they are like new, to become pristine, to revert to their original condition, to adopt an appearance that will satisfy and impress even the most stringent domestic critic. Then she lowers her arms and slumps exhausted into a rocking chair at the very back of the cave, closing her eyes but forgetting to dream.

A Deep Breath

I BLOW A CANDLE out. Then I blow on the thick glowing wick and it bursts into flame. My breath has the power to extinguish and ignite. My lungs or my mouth must be special. I climb the slopes of the volcano to test the limits of my extraordinary ability. I blow down into the crater and the bubbling lava cools to a dim pulsation. I blow a second time and the mountain erupts. I barely escape with my life, but what of that? The city will be destroyed. Next I will blow out the sun. My exhalation will create an eclipse that will last for as long as I choose. The sky grows dark, the endless chill of the cosmos freezes the clouds and they sail overhead like sluggish ships with icicle studded hulls. I will blow the sun back to life. But I am too cold, my teeth are chattering, my breath is a dense fog. I have destroyed the world, but what of that? Light a candle in my memory and that will be more than enough.

The Tired Bed

THE BED WAS TIRED. But the girl was tired too. The bed slept on a bigger bed but tonight she wanted to sleep on that bigger bed. She decided to go to bed before the bed did. When the bed finally went to bed it found that she had taken up all the available space. She was sleeping in a diagonal across the bigger bed and there was no room on the mattress for the small bed. Oh dear! Where would the bed sleep now? On the floor? But no, there was no need for that. The bed said to itself, "I want to sleep on a bed and I am a bed. Why should I not sleep on myself?" This was the best solution. The bed folded itself in half but the half that was underneath also wanted to be on top, so it folded itself again. Once started, the process would never stop. When the girl woke in the morning and blinked her eyes she saw that the smaller bed had vanished. It had folded itself into a dot and then one final time into nothingness. There is no rest for the wicked and even less rest for the implausibly tired and impossibly folded, it would seem. The girl went to town that morning and bought a hammock. She strung it over the bigger bed in case she ever fell out in the middle of the night.

The Illuminations

A MODERN MAN OR woman has a brilliant idea and a lightbulb glows above their heads. But in the olden days it would have been candles instead of bulbs and one of those candle-lit ideas must surely have been the notion of the lightbulb? Then the lightbulb was invented. We can go further back in time to that dim era when we took shelter in caves. A prehistoric man or woman had a brilliant idea and two sticks rubbed together appeared above their heads. The notion of the candle had come to them. We have no idea what the illumination of the future will look like. Perhaps robots will rule the Earth and inspiration will announce itself with a small nuclear explosion directly over their heads, assuming they will even possess heads, which I very much doubt. Meanwhile I sit here in the dark by the open window looking down across the land and a firefly circles my head and I suppose I might invent something modest and simple soon.

The Ostraca of Inclusion

An ostracon is a shard of pottery on which is written the name of one who is destined to be ignored. The democracy of exclusion is at work when the ostraca are gathered and inspected at the end of the day. The process is anonymous; no one else will know whom you have selected for ostracism if you keep your lips sealed. Your ostracon is unidentifiable. But let's not suppose that only the names of living people can be marked on them. We have learned to exclude all things equally.

In a place far from where you are, on the other side of reality, there is an assembly of those characters from all the unwritten stories that can be told in no more than one very deep breath. They are gathering in order to determine which stories will be exiled. The titles are written on ostraca that are then dropped into an urn. The tales that are no longer wanted in that realm seek refuge in our world. But in order to be admitted here they first transform themselves into written texts.

Beyond the Edge

A MAN WAS CROUCHING on the path that runs along the side of the river, and as I approached him I saw he was moving a chess piece in the dust. It was a white knight. I was almost on top of him before he paused and turned to look up at me. Then I asked him what he was doing and he replied that he was playing a game of boardless chess. It had started in a distant city on a regular board, like most chess games, but frustrated with the limited area on which the entire struggle was expected to progress, he had agreed with his opponent to allow pieces to move beyond the boundary squares when necessary. And that is what had occurred.

"My knight kept going," he added, "off the edge and along the streets and out of the city, and I didn't have a desire to turn him around and head back to the board. So here we are, and the game continues, or at least I'm assuming it does, many years later. My opponent might have resigned by now and gone home; or he may have captured my king in my absence and defeated me without me knowing; or he too could be wandering the world with a piece in his hand, moving it across the invisible squares of the land until a stranger stops to ask him about it."

I laughed and bade him have a good day, then I rode around him with due care and cantered towards the small town I saw looming ahead, milky smoke issuing from the chimneys of its houses. As I entered the town and reached the main square, I saw two men playing chess outside a café, and I wondered what might happen if the white knight also came this way and became involved in their game, an unexpected and accidental ally to one side, capturing black pieces as it wandered across the board. The incident could incite a real fight between these players and the newcomer, a three-way battle that would mean broken teeth.

If only that migrating knight was half black and half white, like many actual horses in the world, bloodshed could be avoided. A piebald chess piece is surely neutral. I was tempted to return to the river path and warn the fellow of the hazard ahead, but I had vowed never to retrace my steps. I was fleeing a battle and I too was a knight that had ventured beyond the edge of his board and kept going. Unlike the man crouched in the dust, I had taken precautions, for I had stopped at an abbey and bought a flagon of the darkest ink from the brothers in the scriptorium and had painted on my white stallion the stripes of salvation.

The Book Burning

THERE WAS A COUNTRY where the people thought that petty crime was too petty to pay attention to, and most of them had lives that were far from perfect. Because of their tendency to turn a blind eye to misdemeanours, most of the politicians and officials were openly corrupt, and everyone seemed to get along just fine. Bribery, pilfering, perjury, and simple fraud were commonplace.

Because corruption tends to get worse over time, it wasn't too long before one of these politicians decided that intimidation, kidnap and beatings were acceptable too. He soon grew more powerful than his opponents and many schemers flocked to his banner in order that they might profit. And so the numbers of his followers swelled to the point where he decided to attempt a putsch.

It was successful and this politician was able to declare himself a dictator, the one and only truly inspired leader of the realm, a supreme authority whose word was law. The country became a place where the citizens were too frightened to complain about anything the government did, no matter how drastic or unpleasant. And the dictator in charge always contrived to tighten his control.

Understanding that ideas were his main enemies, he did what autocrats have done throughout the ages and ordered the burning of books. All books without exception. It was a calamity for readers, or at least it seemed that way, when libraries were doused with fuel and they went up in flames. But these infernos were never as spectacular as the dictator thought they should be. He sighed.

The buildings spluttered and went out and collapsed in upon themselves in a way that was rather disappointing. They should have burned all night. But the truth is that the libraries were empty. In a country where people think that petty crime is too petty to pay any attention to, who ever bothers to return a borrowed library book? Nobody. And that was the first failure of the new regime.

Unwanted in Paradise

The word "para" means "beyond", therefore "paradise" must mean "beyond Dise" but where exactly is Dise? It must be another name for our planet, because we are here now, but after we die we will move to Paradise. That's what we are told, so it should be true. But in what language is Dise the name for our planet? Perhaps that of the first human beings who could speak.

I am positive they were interesting people, but let's not worry about them right now. Why was the original name of our planet Dise? I'm going to suggest that it's an antecedent of the word "dice" and that our ancestors understood that the entire world, and all life upon it, is subject to the whims of chance, and that's why they gave such a name to their world. It was a way of acknowledging that the world arose by accident, through a haphazard process of physics. It was a big gamble that we would evolve as we did, a lucky throw of the cosmic dice.

But Paradise is beyond Dise and the rules there are different; it is a place beyond chance. This seems to imply that Paradise is not accidental and random, like Dise is, but that it was deliberately designed. We are led to a conclusion that I don't think any religion has seriously considered before, namely that Paradise was created by God in the same way an architect designs a building, with a great deal of preparation, leaving nothing to chance; but the world we live on arose independently, as if all the chance pushed out of Paradise took revenge on the material universe. Paradise is a product of intelligent design; poor old Dise is a fluke.

We live our accidental lives on an arbitrary sphere in a meaningless universe and when we die we move to the carefully constructed and purposeful realm of God. But the angels don't want us there. We aren't part of the original plan. We are unexpected and uninvited guests. When we arrive we are despised by the winged locals, who refer to us as immigrants in contemptuous tones.

A Room With a View

I LIKE THE OLD wardrobes best, you know, the heavy ones with big oval mirrors that can only be moved by teams of straining men who painfully 'walk' them across rooms and then discover they won't fit through the doors.

Not long ago I had one just like that.

How did they get it inside in the first place? Maybe they built the room around it and the house around the room and the street around the house and the city around the street? Yes, it must have been that way. I don't like the new wardrobes that come in separate pieces and are screwed together.

There's something not quite right about them.

They are insubstantial and too light. I hate hosting them in my corners. I start to itch every time one is pushed against a wall. The floorboards refuse to sag under them. It's like wearing a light cotton shirt instead of a woolly jumper on your back on a cold day. That's a rough equivalent of how it feels. From now on I simply won't tolerate them. I will push them over.

I don't know how I'll manage that but I'll find a way.

The old wardrobes are the best and are welcome inside me anytime. The new ones can go back to where they came from. That's my view and I'm sticking with it. I must be allowed to express my views openly. That's what free speech is about. That's what makes democracy worthwhile. I am a room.

A room with a view.

White Cliffs

His geography teacher was an impatient man who liked to throw the board eraser at pupils who gave the wrong answers to the questions he spat at them. This was in the days when teachers could use a certain amount of physical violence against a child and nobody thought it strange. If a pupil *had* thought it strange, he or she would be beaten for the speculation if they voiced it. Terrible times, really, and Nathan looked back at his school days with utter contempt.

"You boy!" snarled Mr Johnson, his lips glistening. "What are the White Cliffs of Dover made from? Answer me!" And Nathan blinked out of a daydream as the thick finger of the tyrant jabbed in his direction. The answer was obvious, wasn't it? But he felt a pinch of fear as he replied, "Rock, sir."

Mr Johnson rocked back on his heels, the way he always did just before he hurled the board eraser, as if he was generating the necessary momentum through his legs. His voice became less drooly, always a bad sign. "I see we have a clever clogs in the class today. And what happens to a clever clogs?" He cast the board eraser overarm like a cricketer, and Nathan's sternum was the wicket. The missile thudded against his chest with the sound of a fist knocking on a door for immediate admittance. The pain was dull but grew in intensity, a pulsing ache.

"The White Cliffs of Dover are made from chalk!" Mr Johnson bellowed. "From what are they made, boy? Hurry and tell me."

"Chalk, sir!" panted Nathan.

Mr Johnson sighed and paced in front of the blackboard. He had a second board eraser ready in his hand and he now used it to clean the board. Never short of board erasers, was he. As he completed this task, Nathan wondered at how it removed the chalk marks so easily and yet had bounced off his chest without leaving a dent, just a bruise that would heal within a few days. Did this mean that a human chest was more durable than the White Cliffs of Dover? Yes!

The years passed and Nathan left school, went to university, graduated, worked as an engineer. He moved to France, somehow got involved in politics, rose high as an advisor to the government on various large scale engineering projects. Modifying the landscape had become easier than ever before thanks to new technologies. He always walked into meetings with his chest puffed out, his durable chest, vastly stronger than a cliff, a fact he had learned from experience.

His power increased to the point that when history suddenly became very odd, as it often does, he was in a position to benefit. There was a coup and a military regime took over control of France. The rise of Napoleon had been unexpected; an outsider, almost a foreigner, appearing to lead a willing country into war to forge an empire. It was even more surprising in the guise of Nathan, an Englishman willing to assist his adopted country cross the Channel and conquer the old enemy. All previous invasion attempts had failed. But Nathan remembered…

The enormous board eraser was ready within half a year.

Pushed by tugs towards the English shore, capable of rubbing out the White Cliffs as if they had never existed and opening a breach in the armour of the island nation, the board eraser preceded the invasion fleet. "Chalk, sir!" Nathan said to himself under his breath, and then in French, "Craie, monsieur!" Then he laughed in a manner that he wouldn't have dared attempt when he was at school.

Map of Conquest

DID I TELL YOU about that curious situation a few years ago when all the governments in Africa suddenly decided to paint their countries the same colours as on the maps that hung on the walls of palaces, courthouses and schoolrooms? It was a collective madness that began nobody knows where. But soon enough, teams of workers were out in the fields with tins of paint and brushes, or using rollers to turn the slopes of mountains the desired shade, or strolling beaches and spraying the sand with glossy emulsion, and before long nothing was the same as it had been. But the task was big and even the smaller territories of that enormous continent never managed to decorate more than a quarter of their total surface areas.

It's true that different maps published by different cartographers utilise different colours for different countries. Each president or prime minister chose the maps that happened to be hanging on the nearest wall when they made the momentous decision. Some of these maps relied on only four colours for all the nations on the continent, others preferred to be more flamboyant and use five, six, seven or more colours. The paint industry certainly benefited from the increased demand, and many oil tankers were converted to carry acrylic paint instead, simply because the quantities needed could not be imported quickly enough in the standard way. The strangest aspect is how the citizens went along meekly with the scheme.

Perhaps the mood was contagious, the desire for change, for brightening up and reinvigorating landscapes and scenery that were already bright and invigorating. Who knows? The motive is still a mystery, even to those who felt it at the time. Tanzania embarked on painting their entire country grey; Kenya attempted to be purple; Ghana orange; Algeria green; Congo pink. A country that chose to be painted blue would not have to paint most of its rivers. Ethiopia was full of teams of workers with buckets of red paint, and there was no requirement for them to paint the lava lake in the caldera of the Erta Ale volcano. Gabon, dense with forests, would have done well to choose green as their colour, but they went for brown.

The consequences of the cosmetic alteration to the continent were unexpected and extremely serious. A series of events that should have been purely aesthetic but were geopolitical and catastrophic were set in motion the instant the first lick of paint was applied by a brush to the first boulder. The map that hung on the wall of the National Assembly in the city of N'Djamena in the country of Chad showed the country as an irregular yellow shape, a particular shade of yellow the same as that of the desert that comprises the majority of the territory. The painters of Chad had less work to do than the painters in all the other countries. In fact they were told not to bother at all. While other nations toiled, Chad waited and watched.

Then it made a move. Its leaders saw an opportunity that might never come again. That is how one of the poorest and weakest African countries managed to invade and occupy all the others. Now we no longer speak of 'Africa' in the present tense but only in the past, an example from history. We talk instead about the Chadian Empire, a continent-straddling hegemony. They moved decisively and swiftly when everyone else was tired, distracted, absorbed, because large-scale decorative projects have that effect. The house is burning down; we will just finish painting this corner before we attempt to flee. The paintbrush is a shackle. Just one more dab here and there, on this dead tree, on this rotting zebra, on this lost city.

Just A Second

JEFF HAD INVENTED A time machine. He knew it would move him forward in time but he didn't know how far. There was no way of controlling it, but he resolved to be brave and take the chance. He climbed onto the seat and pedalled. Nothing happened. Then he dismounted and shrugged his shoulders.

Nothing at all had changed. It was therefore obvious that the machine didn't work. He checked the circuits and the power source and found they were fine. He frowned and went to fetch a coffee. Then he stopped worrying about it and drank his beverage and left the house to meet his friends. That's the kind of man he was; never concerned too much when things went wrong, just a relaxed person who took his time about any task and abandoned it when it was baffling.

But he never abandoned tasks forever. The following day he mounted the machine again and pedalled. Once more nothing happened and he dismounted. He checked the circuits, discovered they were all in order, and went off to do something else. And thus a pattern was established. He regarded the time machine as a failure but couldn't bring himself to dismantle it. Whenever he passed the device where it stood in the corridor, he would mount and pedal it. He began to think of it as an exercise bike instead of the ingenious physics-defying contraption it was.

What he never learned was that it did work, but only travelled one second into the future when it was operated. A future that is only one second ahead of the present has almost nothing noticeably different about it. This is why Jeff believed the machine to be a failure. But his persistence had an unusual result. Seconds accumulate, turn into minutes, into hours, days, weeks, months. And everyone knows that months become years with little fuss, very little fuss indeed...

And finally, when he was an old man, too tired to pedal the apparatus, which had turned rusty anyway, he sat in his softest chair and thought about his life; and it struck him as curious how he had managed to outlive all his friends and how technology had advanced in such great strides between the time of his birth and the present. Not once did he suspect that he had contributed to any of these strides with the machine parked in the corridor, the willing but slow steed of an unwitting chrononaut, a man who had explored the future without ever realising it.

The Eclipse Flower

THE SUNFLOWER IN JANE'S garden was an unusual one. It was planted in the exact centre of the flowerbed and was an enormous bloom on a long stalk. When she went out in the early morning to drink her coffee on a bamboo chair, the stalk would be drooping to the east, the bloom touching the ground, and very slowly the stalk would straighten itself, pulling into the sky the flower, which would change colour from red to orange to yellow. At noon the bloom would tower high above her and she could bathe in its shadow, which was surprisingly warm on the skin.

As the afternoon progressed, the stalk would begin to sag again, but this time the droop would be towards the west. The huge flower would ripen in colour, darkening, softening, turning a deep russet before touching the ground, where it would come to rest, as if sleeping. What happened after that, Jane couldn't guess. Night in the garden was still a mystery to her. By the time the stars came out, if that's what they did, she would be curled in her hammock and fast asleep. In her dreams, there was no answer to the question. It was always a forbidden secret.

But eventually the mystery was solved. As she basked in the midday shadow of the mighty bloom, a butterfly flitted past her head and then flew up and came to rest on the surface of the flower. Other butterflies joined it. Bees too. Within minutes the entire area of the yellow flower was covered by a mixture of the two kinds of insects and the result was an unintentional eclipse. The differing bodies of the butterflies and bees were like the seas and highlands of the moon. Jane felt a chill and the birds went silent. Then to her astonishment the stars appeared.

They were tiny sunflowers and there were thousands of them. They sprinkled the garden like constellations. Jane was enthralled but knew that eclipses don't last long. She began walking towards one of the tiny flowers but it was much further away than it seemed. It was just an illusion that it was in her garden. The reality was that it was beyond her property. She kept walking, forsaking her home, but it remained tiny. She realised at last that the stars were giant sunflowers too but at vast distances. And now she is lost in the immense spaces between gardens.

Monsieur Choux

When he sat on his favourite chair and ate cakes, he was aware that flakes of pastry often stuck to his beard. He would rise ponderously from his comfort and peer at his face in the mirror over the empty fireplace. It was summer and his cat was moulting. He would flick the flakes away with a deft finger and then carefully brush his beard that was rather too long to be fashionable.

The pastry flakes flew into the corners of the room or went under the table where in the middle of the night a mouse would appear to eat them. The cat would be curled up on the same bed in which the bearded man slept. There was no risk of the mouse being killed and prevented from continuing its work. The flakes would accumulate to an appalling degree without its assistance.

It was a fairly gentle cat anyway and had no hatred for mice. The man was gentle too, apart from when he flicked pastry flakes away, and then he was like an avenging giant. Each time he brushed his beard, a few hairs would come out, pulled from his chin and cheeks by the force of the brush, and these he would scatter over the carpet. He always treated floors as disposal areas.

The cat liked to claw at the carpet and extract individual threads from the weave. At the same time the motion of its paws worked the discarded beard hairs and also its own shed fur into the pattern. This wasn't intentional but it was effective. Over many years, the carpet changed its composition. It began life as a carpet of artificial fibres but was turning into a carpet of hair and fur.

There was more hair than fur in it, to be honest, because the bearded man's face lost more growth in total than did the cat's body. Let's make no bones, he had a large face. Maybe he needed a wife instead of a cat and possibly his beard didn't help him to find one, not that there's anything wrong with beards, but his was just too long and he loved cakes. This has already been said.

His beard also had a little cat fur in it, because the cat liked to rub its head against his chin whenever it had the chance, usually when he was in bed and asleep. And then one day, he realised that the entire carpet was exactly like his beard. It no longer had any artificial fibres left, but was a carpet only of copious beard hair and some fur, a carpet the cat had made over years with its claws.

When a carpet is an analogue of a beard, the things that happen to a beard might also happen to it. This is an ever-present danger. The sky outside the window abruptly darkened and the bearded man got out of his chair to peer out. He saw a colossal man standing in front of the house and this giant's beard was a carpet, mainly of hair with a little cat fur in it, and a flake of pastry too.

The bearded man guessed that this terrible image was only a reflection in a mirror, that the true giant was all around him right now, that his carpet was the real beard. So what was he? A flake of pastry in that beard! Nothing more, nothing less. As the huge fingers came to flick him away, he laughed for the first time in many weeks, but only because he didn't have time to make a speech.

Tumble Keys

SHE HAD LEFT THE keys in her trouser pocket and they went into the washing machine with all the other clothes. This wasn't the first time it had happened, but the rattling noise had always alerted her. When the wash cycle was over she would extract the trousers, grope in the pockets until she found the wet keys and snatch them out. They had never made it as far as the tumble drier.

Until today. For some reason there was no rattle this time. Had she left a napkin or handkerchief in the same pocket? The wet clothes came out of the washing machine and into a basket and were conveyed to the tumble drier. The lid was closed, the timer was set and the gentle rotation spun the laundry in a horizontal whirlwind of warmth. The keys were in there, but she had no idea.

A lock works in a certain way. There are pin tumbler locks that open when the key pins push the spring-loaded driver pins up until their ends are aligned with the shear line, thus allowing the plug to rotate freely. The correct key is needed for the key pins to push the driver pins in the right way. But not every lock is part of a visible door. A few are set into the fabric of spacetime itself.

There was a door to another dimension inside the drum of the tumble drier. As the keys rotated they opened the lock of that door. Whether it was a higher dimension or a lower is unknown. But the clothes fell through from this world and ended up in that one. The trousers with the keys were lost too. When she opened the door, she blinked at nothingness, at an utter absence of clothes.

And in another universe, things that had no earthly use for them carried away the latest batch of garments in single file, laughing in a peculiar way as they did so, and the keys fell from the pocket and were lost unseen on a jungle path that wasn't really a path that led through what wasn't truly a jungle to a place where the clothes would be added to the others in a growing mountain.

Nostalgia City

THERE IS A MEMORY for everyone on every street corner in Nostalgia City. As you walk along the pavements, the sights and sounds and smells evoke a past event in your life that makes you pause, close your eyes and smile, and yet the feeling is not only sweet but tinged with bitterness and ruin too. It is the most potent form of nostalgia, one full of yearning as well as happiness, and that yearning has something deeply melancholy about it, a realisation of loss, the inability to clasp the wisps of the evocation and hold them close enough for more than a few moments.

For this reason, no one is able to rush, and all linger a long time in various parts of the urban labyrinth, sitting on the stone benches in the parks, leaning over the bridges to gaze at the river, blinking at the sunrise or the sunset through gaps in the buildings, feeling the insubstantial weight of the shadows of passing clouds as tender hands on one's brow. The experience of living there is so intense that no one can live there, and the entire population is composed of visitors, transients, people for whom nostalgia is like a glass of wine sipped secretly before dinner.

But nostalgia is a familiar trap as well as a peculiar comfort. Too much erodes the soul, damages the ability of the human organism to appreciate the present in the right way. The *now* becomes merely a search for the *was* and the mind starts to believe that backwards is the proper direction for the inner eye. Nostalgia City is a perfumed and sensuous maze of streets, houses, colonnades, pools, towers, cafes, belvederes, alleys and galleries, but it is stale on a deep level, implacably so. A city without a future is a scented bubble blown from black stagnant water.

Even the city foundations consist of acutely sharpened feelings, no more than that, and the solidity above is only an illusion. We arrive full of hopes, vague desires that are always fulfilled, but the effect is not quite what we imagined. I pass a tree and it fills me with echoes of a summer, a girl, a kiss, and these echoes lap inside my heart with steadily increasing and then diminishing force. Too much of this kind of thing is unbearable. The weeping willow brushes my face and I want to leave and not leave at the same time. The paradox is painful, destructive.

Sooner or later, and generally sooner, a visitor will seek to escape from Nostalgia City. It is impossible to rush even when making a frantic effort to leave. You will drag your suitcase behind you on the cobbles of the street that reminds you of that evening in a summer long ago when you were young and already thinking of a time when you were even younger. Nested nostalgia, flavours within flavours, like sighs and smiles within tears and groans. The suitcase might burst open and scatter your belongings in a setting already strewn with implicative memories.

Beyond the limits of the city we believe we are free at last. But this is not so. The freedom we crave, the freedom from nostalgia, has its own powers of evocation and we are helpless before it.

Everything outside the city, everything that is *not* the city, reminds us of the time before we entered the city, an innocent time, simple and pure, a blessed idyll before we became the unwitting slaves of nostalgia. We are saturated with nostalgia for a time before we were assailed by nostalgia. This is the absurd and bittersweet irony of departure. We will never return.

Freight of Years

THE WAY HE AMUSED himself on bus journeys was by estimating the age of every other passenger and adding them together. Once he had done this, it was just a matter of projecting the total of years into the past and trying to visualise the passing scenery as it was then.

This was fun and continually tested his historical knowledge. He often included his own age in the equation, but was unsure whether this skewed the results. He was fifty years old, so immediately he boarded a bus and it set off, half a century was removed from the surrounding landscape. Cars acquired elegant curves, women pedestrians mainly wore skirts and rarely trousers traffic policemen smiled graciously.

But those occasions when he was the only passenger were uncommon and it was more likely that the bus would be crammed to capacity. Young people did use buses, but the old outnumbered them. It truly amazed him how many millennia could be contained on one vehicle. A bus with seats for forty passengers might easily take him back to the Roman Empire, to Ancient Athens and beyond. A full double-decker coach could even carry him and his febrile brain to Sumer and the very beginning of civilisation. It was an intensely exciting and erudite game.

One morning the bus he intended to catch to a distant city was already full. There was no room for him and it departed without him. He tramped to the train station instead, annoyed at having to pay for a more expensive ticket, but also curious about how this mode of transportation would alter the game. The train was a long one with many carriages. There would be a considerably greater total of years. Enough to deposit him in prehistory among his neolithic ancestors. It was exciting.

He boarded the train and when it pulled out of the station he vacated his seat and wandered through the carriages adding up the years. He was gratified to arrive at a total of three hundred centuries. There would be a selection of long extinct beasts to admire, mammoths among them. Yes, it was fine to travel by train and worth the extra expense! He returned to his seat and pressed his forehead against the glass.

The train entered a long tunnel and nothing at all was visible through the window except the darkness of ignorance, of a time before agriculture and urban society, when communication was oral, when tribes wandered a world without borders, foraging for food, avoiding predators. He waited for the train to emerge again, so that he could see these wonders with his own eyes, a tourist at the dawn of his species...

Out of the tunnel they raced, and sure enough the mammoths loomed over the embankments. But he frowned. There was something wrong. As the mighty beasts lumbered down the slopes onto the track and the brakes of the train squealed in response, he realised these were made from metal. They were mechanical monsters. And now he understood that a freight of years can be projected forwards as well as back.

The Lamp

HE BOUGHT THE THING in a street market and that was a problem because he couldn't take it back and demand the return of his money. The trader had certainly moved on to another location now, for he was the itinerant type and had admitted this at the outset. "I come from far away and tomorrow your city will be the *far away* I come from."

They were curious words spoken in a tone both wistful and defiant. A buyer must beware of such transactions, but the object was something he truly wanted, an example of an outdated futuristic style that both amused him and filled him with nostalgia. He remembered lava lamps when they were fashionable, and now he had one again.

He plugged it in at home but it was a disappointment. Instead of blobs of vibrant colour moving endlessly up and down inside the glass tube and breaking apart and reforming, the lamp merely shone with a dull greenish light and the contents seemed to harden and crystallise. He picked it up to shake it, but no liquid inside moved. Broken?

Perhaps it simply needed to warm up. It was, after all, many years old. The last time lava lamps had adorned the coffee tables of ordinary homes there was fusion jazz on the turntable and trousers widened at the base, a more innocent and garish era. He left it plugged in and went to do chores, then engrossed himself in a book on the sofa.

Once he glanced up and saw that the lamp was changing shape. It was melting and warping, so he disconnected it from the power with a sigh of annoyance, but the green light remained deep within. It must have stored a significant charge inside itself like a battery. He ignored it and returned to his book, the plot of which was fascinating.

The entire narrative seemed to be about to change into something that bore little resemblance to what had transpired so far. This was odd, to say the least, and thrilling. Then he heard a fluttering. His eyes rose out of the page with enormous effort as if extracting themselves from quicksand. He saw the gigantic moth circling the coffee table.

It still contained the green light at the centre of its body and because it is a fact that moths flap around sources of light endlessly, the creature had no choice but to attempt to orbit itself. Then he knew that the trader in the market hadn't cheated him. He had been sold a larva lamp. Such a simple mistake! Aiming carefully, he hurled the book.

The Wardrobe of Love

ARE THERE ANY READERS out there who have felt romantic or erotic desire for a character in fiction? When I was young and read Tolstoy's *War and Peace* I developed a crush on Sonya Rostova, but not on the more obviously alluring Natasha. In recent years I have lusted for Selma from V.S. Naipaul's *A Flag on the Island* and Iris O'Malley from Chester Himes' *Cotton Comes to Harlem*. Strange how it is possible to desire someone who doesn't actually exist! You may reply that it's not at all weird to fall in love with a fictional character, because in the world people often fall in love not with a real person but an imaginary version of them.

That's a good answer and it suggests that love is essentially one sided. Yet I still regard the situation as odd. For example, in an empty wardrobe, any wardrobe, there is a person who doesn't exist. They are standing there right now! They don't exist and never have and never will, and they are inside that wardrobe. In every vital aspect, in shape, size, appetite, health, intelligence, they are no different from the character in a book that we desire. Neither exists. That makes them equivalent. Why don't we fall in love with the contents of empty wardrobes? In other words, why don't we kiss and caress thin air? Why don't we marry an absence?

Because we don't, or at best we very rarely do. That empty wardrobe is absolutely like a book. It contains a person who doesn't exist, just as books do, and in fact it can hold not just one but many nonexistent occupants, again exactly like a book. Why not? People without existence take up no room. A wardrobe can hold a thousand, a million, a billion or more of these nonexistent people, just as easily as it can hold one. And we already know that it does hold one. We know this because it's an empty wardrobe and there is always a nonexistent person inside an empty wardrobe. This has already been proven. I know what you are going to say to t his.

You don't equate fictional characters with thin air. You equate them with concepts, and one can become enamoured of concepts. That's your answer. Yes, I agree, but the idea of a nonexistent person inside a wardrobe is a concept too, and yet you aren't enamoured with *that* one at all. If you were, you wouldn't be reading this right now. You would be rushing up the stairs to the room where your empty wardrobe is located, to throw open the door and kiss the nothingness inside, to hold it close and whisper in its non-ear, because that nothingness is the same as the fictional characters you love in the books you read, who are also nothingness.

I have said enough. I am going to take action, to demonstrate the impeccable logic of my position by embracing the thin air in my own wardrobe. I enter the room, move across the floorboards and approach my reflection in the oval mirror. Then I grasp the door handle and pull. There is a sudden rush of air that is thin no longer. A stampede bowls me over, tramples me underfoot, and only the fact that the feet have no weight prevents me from being flattened into oblivion. All the fictional characters that have ever been desired by readers in the entire history of literature have burst out and made a wild escape over my conceptually bruised body.

The Lost Coffee

I WORK IN THE archives of the library at my local university and coffee is the fuel that keeps me going as the long afternoons drag on. I made myself a cup and was heading back to the tiny office where I catalogue books when I was summoned by one of my assistants. It sounded urgent, so I rested my mug on a shelf, in a gap between missing volumes, and hurried off to attend to the problem.

When I had finished with that business I went to retrieve my coffee. But I couldn't find it. I had failed to take note of its location. There are miles of library shelves and I wandered up and down for about an hour, looking for it without success. In the end I gave up and went to my office. I was acutely aware that a cup of coffee was cooling among volumes on some abstruse subject or other.

This seemed a metaphor for something, but I couldn't decide for what, nor was I able to conclude on the basis of the scanty evidence available to me whether it was an appalling metaphor or a fruitful one. That coffee mug was like a dying explorer who enters a labyrinth and is soon hopelessly lost. He wanders until he is exhausted and gives up at last, and finds a ledge on which to wait.

In future ages some archivist will come across my coffee and give it a catalogue number and maybe even compose a monograph on its attributes. Yes, it will be cold by then, perhaps even solidified. Fossil coffee, the very notion! This idle speculation caused me to sigh. But I had an idea. The Dewey Decimal Classification number for coffee is 641.3373. I know this because I checked.

I hurried out of my office and the books on the shelves became a blur as I ran. At last I found the section that I was seeking. Rows and rows of coffees in mugs, cups or pots, most stone cold, a few lukewarm, some dating back to the dawn of beverages, a selection of coffees that had never been borrowed or consulted. A coffee mausoleum. And somewhere among them, still waiting, my own.

The Möbius Minutes

I work in a department store that sells clothes. I am a clerk and required at meetings to take the minutes. An awful foreboding consumed me before I understood what the task required. No, I wasn't expected to pluck passing time in bunches of sixty seconds from the cosmos. I merely had to record what transpired at those meetings, to note who said what, and why. And it was a great relief when this became clear.

Each meeting began in the same way, with a reading of the minutes of the previous meeting. On the occasion of my first attendance at a meeting I therefore had to read the words of my predecessor, a man still unknown to me. I have been assured that his identity isn't important. No doubt that is what will also be said of me when I am eventually replaced, if that ever comes to pass, which isn't an inevitability.

I stumbled over the words, because they weren't mine, and the formal style in which they were ordered was alien to me. But criticism was mild, I was benignly nodded at and the meeting proceeded. I took careful notes of the exchanges, the arguments and disagreements. I did so in detail, for I wished to redeem myself. The job was essential to my wellbeing, I feared to chance losing it. My notes were copious.

During the second meeting I was required to read my own words, and this time my delivery was a hugely improved performance. I began with a description of my inept previous reading of the minutes. I was praised for the thoroughness of my notes. This encouraged me to be yet more precise in my recording of the meeting's incidents. My pen flew across the paper with a rapidity itself worthy of being noted.

At the third meeting, the reading of the minutes of the second meeting took up more time than the reading of the minutes of the first meeting had taken at the second. This was a natural consequence of greater accuracy. I now was determined to continually improve my performance. Thus at the fourth meeting, my reading of the minutes of the third meeting ate up half the meeting. Yet I considered this a triumph.

It wasn't simply that my minutes became more detailed, but that there was a nesting effect that meant that each reading of the minutes included a description of my reading of the previous minutes. The more meetings I attended, the more these descriptions accumulated. Soon a whole meeting consisted of my reading of the minutes. The executives didn't oppose this but merely extended each meeting's duration.

I assumed they realised that they were trapped in a snare of their own devising and accepted this. A meeting now occupied the full working day and no real business could be conducted. The department store started to lose money, and still none of the executives or managers objected to these constantly growing meetings. I wondered why.

The answer came as I lay awake in bed at home, unable to sleep, mind in turmoil. I knew that within a few months, three at the most, it would no longer be feasible to leave the workplace. I would be stuck in an endless loop of a meeting that would continue through all the nights as well as the days. A prisoner of my own attention to detail.

It would be a permanent meeting, powered by minutes within minutes within minutes, an endless reflection of them. And this reflection held the clue. The department store sold clothes and was full of changing rooms, a series of cubicles in which pairs of mirrors are set facing each other, each pair generating a despicable corridor to infinity.

Endless self-reflection is an essential feature of the business and that's why my superiors made no effort to stop me reading those infernal pages of minutes, and why they will turn to bones listening to them patiently as new owners move in downstairs to take over the building and perhaps fill it with their own obsessive and recursive clerks.

The Mirrors

WHEN HE WAS IN the army he had been ordered to polish his boots until they were like mirrors. It hadn't seemed strange at the time. And now, years later, it was still something he did, and the task gave him a mild pleasure composed of nostalgia and pride.

But finally he had begun to question *why* he did this. After all, it didn't help the boots to walk more efficiently. He stared at his reflection in the toecaps and knew that the sky would find a home there when he put them on and went out. But the sky wasn't always clear, often it was dirty with thick clouds bearing a greasy rain.

Then he wondered what would happen if he polished to excess the real mirrors in his house? Would they too turn into a different kind of object, into boots? He spent many hours on this experiment but the results were disappointing. They remained mirrors, squares, rectangles and ovals of silvered glass that contained in their depths the shelves of books on military history that faced them.

He had proceeded in the wrong direction. A boot must be polished in order for it to turn into a mirror. Therefore a mirror should be neglected, allowed to accumulate grime, before it could be expected to turn into a boot. He stopped cleaning them. The dust thickened. His face in the glass became indistinct, more hazy and distant, as if he had painted his skin with camouflage oils. A domestic commando.

Finally, six months after his decision, he woke one morning and discovered that all the mirrors in his house had vanished, leaving only blank walls. He felt at a loss without them, until he remembered that he could hang his boots in their place. Then he happened to look out of the window. He saw large boots walking by themselves towards the horizon and he knew they were his mirrors, transformed by the alchemy of neglect into sturdy footwear.

The Overdue Book

THE BOOK LAY AT the bottom of the old brass chest that had been in his family for long generations, how many exactly he couldn't even guess, and he had finally set aside an entire afternoon in order to rummage through it. All manner of junk had risen up from its depths, cupped in his hands, as if he was drinking from a pool of mystery that had solidified into clumps of strange shapes. The chest was a large one. He even extracted an early bicycle from it, laying it aside on the bare attic floorboards. And right at the very bottom was the book. He examined it.

A library book, overdue, and he was a foolishly honest man, as he freely admitted to himself, and now the responsibility of returning it became one he couldn't shrug off easily. He wondered at the size of the fine. Maybe he could negotiate with the library staff to pay only a fraction of what was owed. They would be astonished by the mere fact of him returning it, of course, and might possibly dismiss all talk of money. Best not to assume anything until then. He put the book in a bag and slung the bag over his shoulder, then he set off on his long voyage.

First he cycled down to the port on the early bicycle, squeaking all the way as he went and ignoring the strange looks that pedestrians gave him, and when he boarded the ship he left the machine on the quayside for anyone who wanted it. Nobody took it, but he was unaware of this fact as the ferry pulled away from the dockside. The sea was rough beyond the breakwaters and the vessel pitched dreadfully. He clutched the bag close to himself and turned green, the precise shade of the brass chest in his attic. But he had no regrets, not even on the deeps.

Islands passed on starboard and port sides, the stars were intense at night, flying fish skimmed the surface of the dawn water. He felt less sick, sat on deck and let his skin sip the sunlight, the wine dark sea lapping the ship gently now, as if against the sides of an amphora. And then there was land on the horizon and the buildings of an old graceful city reared high and higher. Where in this foreign urban sprawl might the library be located? He had no idea. He would ask people in the street, but would they understand his language? It was worth trying.

He wandered on shaky legs through the streets, still feeling he was on a pitching deck, and nobody could help him. It wasn't the language that was the main problem, but something else. He couldn't identify the obstacle. The day grew old and shadows stretched themselves before bed. At last, tired and dejected, he sat down on a broken wall and sighed. His journey had been wasted, but at least he had made an effort to return the overdue book. Finally an old man approached him, a man with a beard as long as one of the late shadows but pure white.

He listened to the words of the traveller, to his tale and his complaints, and finally he asked to see the book in question. When it was presented to him, he turned it over in his gnarled hands for a few minutes and then carefully unrolled it and squinted in the fading light to read what was written on the parchment, and his back straightened. He now seemed much younger than he was. "One of the lost plays of Sophocles," he said, as he gently returned the scroll. "I am sorry, sir. The Great Library of Alexandria burned down more than two thousand years ago."

About the Author

Rhys Hughes was born in Wales but has lived in many different countries. He began writing at an early age and his first book, *Worming the Harpy,* was published in 1995. Since that time he has published more than fifty other books and his work has been translated into twelve languages. He recently completed an ambitious project that involved writing exactly 1000 linked short fictions. He is currently working on a novel and several new collections of prose and verse.

See his website at https://rhyshughes.blogspot.com/ or follow him at https://www.facebook.com/rhysaurus.

A Request

If you enjoyed this book, its author and publisher would be grateful if you would post a short (or long) review on the website where you bought the book and/or on *goodreads.com* or other book review sites.

Other Books from Recital Publishing

Fabian: A Cubist Biography by Tom Newton
Three Roman Pennies by M.M.B. Higham
A Book with No Author by Brent Robison
Overlook: A Rock & Roll Fable by Paul Smart
The Berserkers by Vic Peterson
The House of the Seven Heavens by Mark Morganstern
Voices in the Dirt: Stories by Ian Caskey
Our Lady of the Serpents by Petrie Harbouri
Voyages to Nowhere: Two Novellas by Tom Newton
The Lame Angel by Alexis Panselinos
The Joppenbergh Jump by Mark Morganstern
Ponckhockie Union by Brent Robison
Seven Cries of Delight and Other Stories by Tom Newton
Saraceno by Djelloul Marbrook
Dancing with Dasein by Mark Morganstern
The Principle of Ultimate Indivisibility by Brent Robison
And please check out ***The Strange Recital***, a podcast about
fiction that questions the nature of reality.

9 798988 670230